Wilbur F. Bryant

The Blood of Abel

Wilbur F. Bryant

The Blood of Abel

ISBN/EAN: 9783337392406

Printed in Europe, USA, Canada, Australia, Japan

Cover: Foto ©Andreas Hilbeck / pixelio.de

More available books at **www.hansebooks.com**

THE BLOOD OF ABEL

TO THE MEMORY OF

WILLIAM LEARNED MARCY,

A DEMOCRAT OF THE OLD SCHOOL; A STATESMAN OF
SUPERLATIVE ABILITY; THE CONTEMPORARY OF
CALHOUN, CLAY AND WEBSTER; AND THE
PEER OF THEM ALL; AND, BEST OF ALL,
THE FEARLESS AND UNCOMPROMISING
DEFENDER OF THE RIGHTS OF
AMERICANS ABROAD,

THIS LITTLE VOLUME IS DEDICATED

BY

THE AUTHOR.

PREFACE.

THOMAS PAINE says, somewhere, that the last part of a book, to be written, is the preface. He might have added, that it was the hardest to write. It is the author's apology to the reader. I do not like apologies. Hence I shall offer none. This little book was not written for gold or for glory, nor for that fool's gold of fame—notoriety. Its author had a word to speak; and he has spoken it.

W. F. B.

WEST POINT, *March 21, 1887.*

"RIEL. was the John Brown of the half-breed,—a fanatic with a just cause behind him, at least a cause which rested on the bed-rock of justice in the minds of his supporters." —[*Springfield Republican.*

"He was a man of strange temperament,
 Of mild demeanor, though of savage mood,
Moderate in all his habits, and content
 With temperance in pleasure, as in food,
Quick to perceive, and strong to bear, and meant
 For something better, if not wholly good;
His country's wrongs, and his despair to save her,
Had stung him from a slave to an enslaver."
            —[*Description of Lambro in Byron's Don Juan.*

"I did all I could to get free institutions for Manitoba. They have those institutions to-day in Manitoba, and try to improve them, while myself who obtained them, I am forgotten as if I were dead."
            —[*Louis Riel's Address to the Jury.*

"Ah God! that gastly gibbet! how dismal 'tis to see
 The great, tall, spectral skeleton, the ladder, and the tree."
            —[*Aytoun.*

"Had Don Pacifico been naturalized at Gibraltar instead of having been born there, he would have been not the less entitled to 'British Protection.'"
            —[*Sir Alexander Cockburn.*

"Speak, Satire, for there's none can tell like thee,
 Whether 'tis folly, pride, or knavery,
 That makes this discontented land appear
 Less happy now in times of peace, than war." —[*Defoe.*

"' My charges upon record will outlast
　　The brass of both his epitaph and tomb.'
' Repent'st thou not,' said Michael, ' of some past
　　Exaggeration? Something which may doom
　　Thyself if false, as him if true? Thou wast
　　Too bitter—is it not so?—in thy gloom
　　Of passion?' ' Passion!' cried the phantom dim,
' I loved my country, and I hated him.' "

　—[*Dialogue between Michael and Junius, in Byron's Vision of Judgment.*

" The watchful care and interest of this Government over its citizens are not relinquished because they are gone abroad, and if charged with a crime committed in the foreign land, a fair and open trial, conducted with a decent regard for justice, and humanity, will be demanded for them."

　—[*President Cleveland's Message to Congress, December 6, 1886.*

" And the Lord said to Cain : Where is thy brother Abel? and he answered : I know not; am I my brother's keeper? And he said to him : What hast thou done? The voice of thy brother's blood crieth to me from the earth."

　　　—[*Genesis, Chap. iv., 9–10.*

THE BLOOD OF ABEL.

PART THE FIRST.

ULTIMA THULE.

THE BLOOD OF ABEL.

PART THE FIRST.

—

THE NORTH-WEST.

"This king of the solitudes needs an empire for his operations."
—[*Professor Bryce.*

THE most important physical division of the North
American continent is the great central plain which
stretches from the Arctic Ocean, on the North, to the Gulph
of Mexico, on the South. This plain is bounded on the West
by the Rocky Mountains, and on the East by the Appalachian
Mountain system, which, under the various names of Appalachian, Alleghany, Catskill, Adirondacks, Green Mountains
and White Mountains, extends along the coast of the Atlantic,
northerly, to the water system formed by the Great Lakes and
the Saint Lawrence River, north of which system the great
plain, leaping beyond the boundaries Nature has fixed in the
South, stretches out, toward the East, to Hudson Bay, and
South of that bay, in the dreary, fan-shaped desert of northern Labrador, which country is bounded on the South by the
Wotchish Mountains. It is hardly exaggeration to say, that
a person might walk through this plain, from the mouth of
the Mackenzie River, at its northern to the Delta of the Mississippi at its southern extremity, without meeting a perceptible rise upon the face of the country. Near the centre of

this basin, however, in about latitude 50° north, there is a broad but gentle swell, without any defined crest. This water-shed, as it is called, starts from the eastern slope of the Rocky Mountains, and runs eastward, toward Lake Superior, a little West of which it divides. Its rise is so gradual, that the unscientific observer can discover the summit, only by the general course of the rivers, which, diverging at this place, like the rivers of Eden, flow in a northerly or southerly direction, toward the Arctic Ocean or the Gulph, accordingly as they rise to the North or South of the summit. It might be shaving the edge of hyperbole to imagine two drops of rain falling upon the summit of this swell simultaneously, and parting company at the apex of its obtuse angle; the one to be borne southward, by the Mississippi, to the tepid waters of the Gulph; the other by Nelson River and Hudson Strait to the frozen ocean of the North. This terrene wave of demarcation was once believed to be the track of the isothermal line of agriculture, in this region. But here history has given the lie to science.

The country north of the 55th degree of latitude may, perhaps, be regarded as the finest fur-producing country in the world. Its rocky soil and severe climate render it unfit for agriculture. The territory lying south of this latitude, and north of the 49th degree, between the Rocky Mountains, and the 89th meridian of longitude, is a country bearing in its womb giant possibilities. Already a large portion of it has been redeemed from desolation and savagery by the silent, but telling labour of the rustic toiler. Fate has destined this to be the great wheat-producing country of the globe. It requires neither the pen of a poet, nor the eye of a seer to picture a second Odessa springing up on the coast of Hudson Bay, when the beaten path of commerce shall lie between the mouth of the Mersey and the mouth of the Nelson. In this country we might place Austria-Hungary, England and France; and have left sufficient territory for a respectable empire. The careful student of history will never consider its climate as militating against its future. Any person familiar with Cæsar's Commentaries will realize what changes the settlement of the country, the cultivation of the soil, and the introduction of civilization have wrought in the climate of Europe. Manitoba is in the same latitude as the southern part of England. Yet the time was, since the commencement of our era, when England, then a cold and barren land, was in possession of wandering tribes who inhabited rude huts, made of wicker and mud, erected in clusters or hamlets, like Indian tipis. One such there was upon the shores of a river, bounded on three sides by a trackless forest. This was called Llyn-Din, or "the town on the lake." Contrast it with the London of to-day.

The pride of the North-West is its rivers and lakes. In these it rivals almost any country of the Old World. For the purposes of this volume the description of only one of these rivers is necessary. The Saskatchewan is geographically and historically famous, at once the Rhine and Tiber of the North-West. Its name is either a corruption of, or a derivative from, the Indian word Kissiskachewan, signifying, in the Cree language, "swift current." This river, like the Nile, has an upper course, consisting of two branches. The North branch rises in Glacier Lake, a body of water, about ten miles in length by two in width, lying on the east slope of the Rocky Mountains, near Sullivan's Peak, at an altitude of 6,347 feet above the level of the sea, nearly the height of Mount Washington. The course of this stream is East, past Mount Murchison, a point of land 15,789 feet above the sea-level—a trifle higher than Mount Blanc. Then, changing its course to a more northerly direction, it unites with the south branch near longitude 105° 12′, about 12° 18′ east of its source. This branch is about 550 miles in length, longer than the Penobscot, Androscoggin and Mohawk rivers combined. The south fork is formed by the junction of two little mountain streams, the

Bow and Belly. In fact, later explorations have nearly established the fact, that the Bow is the main stream; and the other is a mere tributary. Bow River takes its rise in a tiny lake which descends from a magnificent glacier, and in a group of springs in the vicinity. After its junction with the Belly it pursues a southerly course till it unites with the Deer River. Thence it pursues a more easterly course till it unites with the north branch. The latitude of these sources differs a little more than two degrees. From the union of the north and south branches, the main stream pursues its course for about 200 miles. This course is North-East to parallel 54°; then the river, changing its course, describes an ox-bow, takes a general south-easterly course to Cedar Lake. The lake is simply an expansion or widening of the river, which keeps its course to Lake Winnipeg, into the north-west portion of which it empties. In the north-east part of this lake the Nelson River takes its rise; and, after a course of 350 miles, it enters Hudson Bay. This river is, by many geographers, considered an extension of the Saskatchewan. English explorers bestowed the name of the hero of Trafalgar upon the river; but its source has a less romantic name— Winnipeg signifying, in Algonquin, "dirty water." The mountains along the Saskatchewan are heavily timbered. Coal and iron have been discovered upon both branches. The area of the entire basin is 240,000 square miles, larger than the states of California and Minnesota combined. In the year 1876 an American of some pretentions wrote of this valley: "The basins of both branches are generally too wild and mountainous, and the climate too rigorous to admit of much cultivation."

One can not read such words now, and suppress a smile. The valley of the main river presents an excellent agricultural and grazing district. The Saskatchewan is generally frozen from the middle of November till the middle of April. During the greater part of the year, however, it is navigable for steamboats; and is destined to be the great natural thoroughfare of commerce in the North-West.

As the Saskatchewan is to be the greatest natural, so is the Canadian Pacific railroad to be the greatest artificial highway of this country. This company was incorporated February 17, 1881, with an authorized capital of $100,000,000. The charter conferred, amongst other powers, the right of constructing and operating telegraphic lines; the right of building branch roads along the entire length of the main line; and of establishing steamship lines at its termini. The company was subsidized, by the Dominion Government, in the sum of $25,000,000 together with a donation of 25,000,000 acres of land. The government, having previously gone into the railroad business, had constructed 713 miles of road, at a cost of $35,000,000, which it transferred to the company, free of cost. At the session of the Dominion Parliament for 1884, the administration then in power, under the Right Honourable Sir John A. Macdonald, as premier, stood pledged before their constituencies for an early construction of the road. The railroad company was upon the ragged edge of bankruptcy. They could raise money neither in Wall Street nor London, upon the company's bonds. If they failed in the construction of the road, defeat threatened the government. In this dilemma the Van Buren of Canadian politics was equal to the emergency. He resorted to what politicians call "log-rolling." His party, under his leadership, subsidized local roads, and resorted to "every wile that's justified by honour,"—and some which casuists might question,— until they secured the grant of $30,000,000, taking as security a mortgage upon the road from Calendar (near the source of the Matawin River) westward. The opposition characterized the security as absolutely worthless, because the first one thousand miles of the mortgaged track passed through an unproductive country. Considering all things, the establishment of this great highway was cheaply purchased. Whatever faults he may have (and faults he has in profusion), the name of Sir John A. Macdonald is forever linked with the consummation of this enterprise.

In 1885 the capital stock of the road was reduced to $65,000,000. Upon this amount the government has guaranteed a minimum dividend of three per cent. by the year for ten years from August, 1883, the company placing collateral in the hands of the government, which at four per cent. interest, provides for this. The Canadian Pacific extends from Montreal 2,609 miles to New Westminster, in British Columbia. It must be confessed (however reluctantly by us Americans), that the route by the Canadian Pacific Railroad has some advantages in its favour, as against the Union Pacific and Central Pacific, by Omaha and Ogden, to San Francisco. What these advantages are it is foreign to the purpose to enumerate. But the establishment of a branch road from the main line of the Canadian Pacific to the mouth of the Nelson River, and a line of ocean steamers from thence to Liverpool, would be almost the creation of a New World in the North-West. What the Canadian Pacific has already achieved for this country there is not space to write of. It would be the oft-repeated story of towns springing up, like the Ivy of Jonas; of town-sites playing the *role* of Aladdin's Lamp; and, last, but not least, the sturdy tiller of the soil— the man who comes to stay—following in the wake of the speculator.

The Third Napoleon spoke of what he called " the logic of events." One fond of studying this kind of logic might trace a visible connection between the history of the Oregon question, and the building of the Canadian Pacific Railroad. By the treaty of 1818, between Great Britain and the United States, the parallel of 49° north was established as the boundary line between the States and British America, East of the Rocky Mountains, as far as the Lake of the Woods; and a compromise was effected as to the Pacific slope, leaving it

open to the subjects of both the realm and the republic, con-
stituting it a kind of political No-Man's-Land. The march
of civilization forced the question of its ownership upon the
diplomates and statesmen of both nations. Great Britain
limited her claim by the parallel of 42°; and the demagogues
of the Clay and Polk campaign pushed the American claim
to the extravagant and imaginary boundary of 54° 40'.
"Fifty-four forty or fight" was made the slogan of the
democrats, who were led to victory by Polk and Dallas.
President Polk, in his inaugural address, spoke of the American claim as "clear and unquestionable." Had this claim
been successfully asserted, as it was sought to be, Great Britain would have had no coast-line in this region; and the Canadian Pacific Railroad would never have been built, as the
cause for its building would not have existed; and the North-
West would never have been blessed with this great civilizer,
the source of nearly all its prosperity.

In the portion of country last defined there are three entire
political divisions, and parts of two others. The province
of Manitoba lies wholly within this tract. Manitoba has an
area of about 125,000 square miles, being nearly the size of
the states of Minnesota and Wisconsin combined. Manitoba
is bounded on the South by the United States (Minnesota and
Dakota), on the West by Assinniboia and Saskatchewan, on
the North by Saskatchewan and Keewatin, and on the East by
Keewatin. Manitoba is (this is said reverently) the Promised
Land of the North-West. Though neither literally, nor, perhaps, figuratively a "land flowing with milk and honey," it is
a land blessed with a fertile soil, a dry and healthy climate, and
an intelligent and enterprising populace. This province be-
longs to the Dominion of Canada; and is represented in the
House of Commons, at Ottawa, by six members. Manitoba,
along with the remainder of the Dominion, enjoys a government in form monarchial, but in fact republican. We of the
States have been so much impressed by the froth and the

spread-eagleism of the average Fourth-of-July orator, that we have almost come to think that there is no liberty outside of the United States. This is a great mistake. The liberty we now enjoy is very little of it distinctively American. It may, rather, be called Anglo-Saxon, the common property of Englishmen and Americans. Yes, many of the stereotyped axioms of our law, and some of our constitutional enactments are almost literal translations of *Magna Charta.*

In Manitoba suffrage is well-nigh universal. The assertion is ventured, that a person moving across the line from Minnesota to Manitoba, would not experience a perceptible abridgement of his political rights, after he had resided there the requisite period; and had taken the oath of allegiance.

It may be said, that the whole British Empire is taxed to keep up a family of do-nothings, who, save for their empty rank, would not attract the attention of their next-door neighbours. The first part of this proposition is hardly true; the second may be correct; and yet will not the long line of England's monarchs, from William I. to Victoria, compare favourably with our list of presidents? Is not the percentage of greatness as large in the one, as in the other? Then, too, does royalty cost more than our quadrennial presidential elections? It is not meant to convey the idea, that the writer of this volume is a monarchist. But he bases his belief of republicanism on other grounds than those mentioned.

The city of Winnipeg, the capital of Manitoba, is located upon the Red River of the North. This river takes its rise in the United States, and empties into Lake Winnipeg. The city is situated at the junction of the Assinniboine with Red River. Its site is upon a perfectly level plain, between 600 and 700 feet above the level of the sea. It is hard to place the population of a western town, on account of its continued tendency to outstrip itself. But that of Winnipeg may be placed at the approximate figures of 20,000. The city has a system of horse-cars; and is lighted with electricity. In commercial importance Winnipeg is ranked as the fifth city of the Dominion. Winnipeg has steamboat connections, by way of the Red River of the North and Lake Winnipeg, with the mouth of the Saskatchewan, which is navigable for steamboats for hundreds of miles of its course. The Assinniboine is navigable by steamboats for about 300 miles West from Winnipeg; but the Canadian Pacific Railroad has rendered navigation in this direction in less demand.

To speak further upon the numerous attractions of this lovely province would be too great a departure from the purpose of this volume.

Within the extent of territory last defined, and to the West, North and North-West of the province of Manitoba, lie the four new districts of Athabasca, Alberta, Saskatchewan and Assinniboia. These districts were erected out of the North-West Territories, by an order in Council, for sundry purposes, more particularly postal facilities.

The district of Assinniboia is about 95,000 square miles in extent, stretching through three degrees of latitude, and nearly ten degrees of longtitude, and is bounded as follows: On the South by the international boundary line, between the United States and the Dominion of Canada, being the 49th parallel of latitude; on the East by meridian 101⅓, being the western boundary line of Manitoba; on the North by the 9th correction line of the Dominion survey, the southern boundary of Saskatchewan, nearly identical with the 52d parallel; on the West by the eastern boundary of Alberta, at and along the 111 1-5 meridian. The name of this territory is of Indian origin. All of this district lying east of the 104th parallel is included, together with a portion of Manitoba, in a vast plateau, comparable in extent to one of the steppes of Russia. This great table-land has a mean altitude of 1,600 feet, and a width of 250 miles on the international boundary line. Its area is about 105,000 square miles. The district is traversed, from East to West, by the Canadian Pacific Railway. Along

2

the line of the road are located the famous Bell farm, and the settlement of croifters from the Gorden-Cathcart estate, known throughout the world as the Benbecula colony. In this district is situated the town of Regina, capital of the North-West Territories. A little to the north of Regina lies Long Lake. The north-western portion of the district is traversed by the south fork of the Saskatchewan River; the eastern portion by the Qu'Apelle and Assinniboine.

The district of Saskatchewan extends through three degrees of latitude and ten of longitude, and contains about 114,000 square miles. It is bounded on the South by Assinniboia and Manitoba; on the East by Manitoba, Lake Winnipeg and the Nelson river; on the North by the 18th correction line of the Dominion land-survey into townships, near the 55th parallel; and on the West by the line of that survey dividing the 10th and 11th ranges of townships, west of the fourth initial meridian, at and along the 111 1-5 meridian, the same being the eastern boundary of Alberta. This district is traversed by the Saskatchewan River, from which its name is derived. It is sparsely settled, but is a country of immense resources. It contains the settlements of Prince Albert and Battleford— the former located upon the left bank of the north fork of the Saskatchewan about 25 miles from its union with the south branch; the latter upon the right bank of the same fork about 150 miles higher up the stream, at the junction with its tributary, the Battle River. Each of these places is a station of the mounted police, so-called. Between these two stations, a little nearer to the former than to the latter, is a bend in the river, called the elbow. Upon the right bank of the north branch of the Saskatchewan, about 48 miles from its union with its fellow are the town and fort of Carlton. A line drawn nearly due South from hence, fourteen miles to the south fork, would intersect Batoche, a village, the nucleus of a half-breed settlement. About half-way betwixt these two places, seven miles from either, is Duck Lake. A proper understanding of what is to follow demands, that the geography of this region be minutely given; but further details will be given in the relation of events connected therewith.

The district of Alberta extends from the International boundary line, through six degrees of latitude, to the 55th parallel. It is bounded at the South by the United States; on the East by Assinniboia and Saskatchewan; on the North by the 18th correction line, before mentioned; on the West by British Columbia. This district is a namesake of the late Prince Consort. As Manitoba is destined to rival, and, perhaps, exceed Russia as a wheat-producing country, so is Alberta fated to outstrip Switzerland as a dairy-land. Both forks of the Saskatchewan take their rise in this district. The Canadian Pacific Railroad crosses it in the southern portion.

The district of Athabasca lies north of Alberta, which forms its southern boundary. It is bounded on the East by the meridian that forms the eastern boundary of Alberta and the Athabasca and Slave rivers; on the North by the 32nd correction line, near the 60th parallel; and on the West by British Columbia, meridian 120. Athabasca signifies, in the Indian tongue, "swampy." This is no misnomer. The famous Peace River traverses this district. Like Saskatchewan, this district is a country of a thin population, but immense resources.

In the year 1885 the North-West Territories, which included the four districts enumerated, were under the government of a Lieutenant-Governor and Council. This Lieutenant-Governor received his appointment from, and by authority of the Governor-General (of the Dominion) in council. His commission was issued under the Great Seal of Canada; and he held his office during the pleasure of the Governor-General—which meant the pleasure of the administration in power. He administered his government under instructions given him by order in council; or by the Secretary of State. In case of absence, illness, or other inability of the Lieutenant-Governor, the Governor-General was empowered to appoint an administrator (so-called) to execute the functions of the office.

The Lieutenant-Governor's auxiliary council consisted of several persons, not exceeding the number of six, in the first instance, of which council the stipendiary magistrates, for the North-West Territories, hereinafter mentioned, were members, each one by virtue of his office; and each member of such council, whether a stipendiary or otherwise, received his appointment by warrant, under seal, from the Governor-General, with the advice of the Queen's Privy Council for Canada. The Governor, also, appointed a clerk for such council.

As soon as the Lieutenant-Governor was satisfied, that any district or portion of the North-West Territories, not exceeding an area of one thousand square miles, contained a population of not less than one thousand inhabitants of adult age, exclusive of aliens and unenfranchised Indians, he was required to erect that portion into an electoral district, designating by proclamation its name and boundaries. Such district was thereafter entitled to elect a member of the council.

A person to be a qualified elector, to vote for a member of the council, must be a male resident in good faith, and a house-holder of adult age, within the electoral district; and must have resided in such electoral district for twelve months consecutively just prior to the issuance of the writ of election. Aliens and unenfranchised Indians were excepted from the above provisions, by special mention. Any person entitled to vote might be a member of the council.

When the number of elected members amounted to twenty-one, the council was to cease and determine; and such members thereafter were to constitute a legislative assembly.

The Lieutenant-Governor and council were authorized under certain restrictions, to pass ordinances for the government of the North-West Territories. They were further empowered to locate the capital of the North-West Territories, and to change its location, in their descretion.

The Lieutenant-Governor received a yearly stipend of $7,000, which was paid out of the revenue fund of Canada.

The Governor (of the Dominion) might from time to time, by commission under the Great Seal, appoint one or more fit and proper persons (not exceeding three) barristers-at-law, or advocates of five-years' standing, in any of the provinces, to be and act as stipendiary magistrates within the North-West Territories, who should hold office during pleasure, and who should reside at such place or places as might, from time to time, be ordered by the Governor in council. A stipendiary magistrate, as the name imports, is a magistrate who receives a stipend, or pecuniary compensation, for his official services. He is so designated, in contra-distinction of a justice of the peace, who receives no pay whatever. In the North-West Territories the salary of a stipendiary magistrate was fixed, by law, not to exceed the sum of $3,000.

Two of the then incumbents were the Honourable Hugh Richardson, who resided and still resides at Regina, Assinniboia; and Honourable Charles Rouleau, who lived at Battleford, now domiciled at Calgary, Alberta. Both of these gentlemen are lawyers of learning and good standing, as well as gentlemen of recognized ability and refined culture.

Each stipendiary magistrate had the magisterial and other functions appertaining to a justice of the peace, or any two justices of the peace, under any laws and ordinances which might, from time to time, be in force in the North-West Territories; they, also, had power to hear and determine any charge against any person, for any criminal offense, alleged to have been committed in the North-West Territories, or in any territory eastward of the Rocky Mountains wherein the boundary between the provinces of British Columbia and the North-West Territories had not been officially ascertained, as follows:

1. In cases of commission or attempt to commit larceny, embezzlement, or obtain money or property by false pretenses, or feloniously receiving stolen property, in any case where the value does not, in the opinion of the magistrate, exceed two hundred dollars.

2. Cases of aggravated and malicious assault.

3. Assaults upon females (except with intent to commit a rape), and upon males under fourteen years of age.

4. Escape, or assault on magistrates.

In all the cases above named the charge was tried in a summary way, and without the intervention of a jury. In all other criminal cases the stipendiary magistrate and a justice of the peace, with the intervention of a jury of six, might try any charge, against any person or persons, for any crime.

A person convicted of any offense punishable with death might appeal to the Court of Queen's Bench of Manitoba, which had jurisdiction to confirm the conviction or order a new trial. The procedure upon such appeal was regulated by the ordinance of the Lieutenant-Governor in council.

The question of whether or not the common-law right of a defendant as to being tried only upon the presentment of a grand jury, or coroner's inquest, in a criminal prosecution, existed in the North-West Territories was formerly a mooted question amongst lawyers. But it was, in that historic year, forever put at rest. The Queen's Bench of Manitoba, in an opinion full of that specious and plausible reasoning, which intoxicates the understanding, and seduces the judgment, have decided in favour of the negative. The decision in Queen against Connor, decided at Easter Term, 1885, though colourable reasoning, is bad law.

The naturalization laws are particulary liberal. Three years of consecutive residence, and the oath of allegiance, is all that is required. No abjuration is demanded, as with us, and this last is a useless refinement of barbarism.

In becoming a British citizen, the denizen has one thing to

console him: He has sworn allegiance to an empire that is historical in defense of her citizens in foreign lands. If she has murdered sepoys, and oppressed Zulus, let her plead guilty before the Great Tribunal of mankind, or stand her trial. But, if she has maltreated her own subjects, she has not allowed others to do so. In this respect she is the peeress of any nation since the days of ancient Rome.

The law in regard to the property rights of married women is, perhaps, more liberal than that of any state in the American Union. An analysis of its provisions, however, would be foreign to the purpose of this volume.

The system of land surveys and entries is similar to that in force in the western states. The public lands are open to entry under homestead, pre-emption and timber-culture laws. The land is surveyed into sections and townships. So exact has been the survey, that the surveyors have gone over the work twice with chains of different lengths; and the length of north and south township boundaries has been made to conform to the circumfricity of the earth.

The inhabitants of this region are made-up from three general classes—whites, Indians and half-breeds. I think it was Doctor Strauss who compared the American Nation, with its ceaseless tide of immigrants, to a seething smelting-pot, into which are constantly thrown new and crude materials which keep up the heterogeneousness of the entire mass. The simile would not be out of place here.

The whites of the North-West are made-up of Englishmen, Scotchmen, Irishmen, Welchmen, Orcadians, Frenchmen, Icelanders, Canucks; and, indeed, (with scarcely a hyperbole) of every kindred and tongue under Heaven. Their number is uncertain. An author who attempts to give the population of a western territory is in danger of being laughed-at; and being informed, in the vernacular of the day, that he is "behind the times."

The Indians of Manitoba and the North-West Territories

number about 34,000. Most, if not all of these, belong to
the Algonquin family. They are divided into about twenty
different tribes and parts of tribes. A detailed account of
these would be too much of a digression. The Blackfeet, or
Blood Indians, and the Crees are, perhaps, the most important.

The Blackfeet are the most westerly tribe of the Algonquin family. They have a dialect which differs almost radi-
cally from that of the other tribes of the same family. Their
original home was the valley of the Saskatchewan. Intes-
tine feuds caused a separation between the Satiska, or Blackfeet proper, and the Kenna or Blood Indians. The former
retired to the valley of the Missouri. Here they were
dubbed "Blackfeet," by their new-found enemies, the Crow
Indians. They are, by a second secession, now divided into
three bands. These Indians are great horse-thieves. They
are, or at least were, originally, worshipers of the sun; and,
like the Parsees of Persia and India, who worship the same
deity, they never bury their dead. Their number within the
British lines is estimated at 6,000; but this is a little uncertain.

Of the Crees and other tribes, more will be said hereafter.

The term half-breed, as used in the North-West, is applied
generally to all inhabitants of a mixed origin, and particularly
to those of a mixed Indian and Caucasian descent. At the date
of the formation of the territories they contained the representatives of fourteen civilized nations, and twenty-two Indian
tribes. Marriages (mostly of a morganatic nature) were contracted between the civilized men and the savage women.
The amalgamation of the antediluvian days was repeated.
The sons of God seeing the daughters of men, that they were
fair, took to themselves wives of all which they desired. The
Scripture says, that there were giants in those days. So, too,
the half-breeds are a race of large, well-formed and powerful men. Most of them are dark-skinned, though some of

them are fair. They are instinctively travellers. If there is anything in the science of phrenology, the half-breeds of the North-West must, as a rule, have a morbid development of the organ of Locality. They possess many of the Indian characteristics, both as regards instincts and vices. One of the former is the ability of steering across the trackless waste of prairie and forest, and striking an objective point, without any knowledge, save a general one, as to the lay of the country. They are, almost exclusively, without education. They nearly all sign their mark. Like the Indian, they enjoy a good time, and are bent upon having one whenever the opportunity offers. Most of the half-breeds are descended from either Scotch or French fathers. The French half-breeds are, like their paternal ancestry, polite and hospitable.

Harriet Beecher Stowe calls the Anglo-Saxons the Romans of the nineteenth century; and adds that, like the Romans, we over-ride and oppress weaker races; and she mentions, as example, the Negro, the Hindoo, and the North American Indian. She failed to mention the Irishman. Perhaps before this book is closed the reader may conclude that there are others which might have been added to the list.

For a long time, perhaps ever since the separation of the North American colonies from Great Britain, there have existed two' parties in the United States. This is not intended to apply to politics alone. In literature, etiquette, social life, philosophy, and even theology, there have been the two extremes. On the one hand have been the people affected with Anglo-mania; on the other, those suffering from Anglo-phobia. Of course, all are not affected equally with the one or the other of these diseases. There are degrees in this, as in nearly everything else. The first extreme is represented by Dorman B. Eaton; the second is (or, rather, was before reason was dethroned) represented by George Francis Train. The first tries to reproduce England in giant miniature, if that is not a contradiction of terms; the second burns everything "from England but her coal." The one is a mimetic ape; the other a raving mad-man. There is, between the two, a golden mean.

It is this mean we shall endeavour to strike in speaking of England's colonial possessions. In the extent of these England resembles Rome more than in any other respect. The study of the two systems, and a parallelism drawn between the two, might furnish work for a life-time, and a comparison between them is a striking illustration of the superiority of Christian over pagan civilization.

It is hard to find, even in the Autocrat of All the Russias, a stronger example of an absolute despot than was the governor of an ancient Roman province. He united in his person the three primary elements of all government—the legislative, judicial and executive. The Roman citizen only possessed the right to appeal to Cæsar, from the decision of the provincial tyrant. The speech of Honourable William E. Gladstone, upon the Don Pacifico case, depicts this privileged class in its true light. Then the distinction between subject and citizen was even more marked than now. To be a mere subject of Rome meant few of the rights of modern citizenship, except the onerous one of paying taxes, from which the citizen was exempt. The relative judicial rights of the provincial subject and citizen can not be better illustrated than in the trials of Christ and Paul. The former was apprehended, twice hurried from one jurisdiction to another; summarily tried, put to the torture, condemned and executed—all in the short space of twelve hours. On the other hand, Paul, the fortunate native of a free city, saved his back from the torturer's lash by the talismanic sentence: "I appeal unto Cæsar."

Rome acquired her provinces through the double avenue of conquest and bequest, or device by will. Thus Carthage, Sicily and Gaul were conquered; while Bythinia, Cyrene and Egypt were bequeathed. After the acquisition of any province the first thing which Rome sought was the destruction of anything like political unity. She weeded out, with a jealous hand, every *imperium in imperio.* The Achaian League was abolished. Such a thing as a provincial senate was unknown. The few exceptions which existed under the empire may be characterized as mere *umbrae parliamentorum,**—to paraphrase the expression of Tacitus in regard to one of Rome's client princes. Rome treated a conquered province exactly as the late Charles Sumner desired to treat the southern states of the American Union after the Slave-holders' Rebellion—like so many acres of land, and so many millions of people. In the case of Macedonia, disregarding ancient land-marks, Rome divided the province into four arbitrary and isolated fractions, forbidding the inhabitants of different provinces to intermarry, or even to hold landed property in more than one of the four provinces. It was the usual custom to give a province to a bankrupt political hack, in order that he might retrieve his lost fortunes with rapine and pillage. Such extravagances as characterized Hastings and Eyre, and excited the just condemnation of the civilized world, were the day's doings with Roman proconsuls.

In the provincial government of Great Britain there is much, perhaps, to criticise, but censure will be reserved for the nonce. It is true, that in the frontier provinces of Her Britannic Majesty the three functions of government are not well-defined. Then, too, in the North-West Territories, by legislative enactment—or, rather, by judical interpretation thereof,—the common-law right of a trial by twelve jurymen is denied. The right of the defendant in a criminal case, to be tried only upon the presentment of a grand jury, has also been denied to persons charged with the commission of offenses, in these territories by the same interpretation. As has been stated before, the right of a trial by jury has been absolutely dispensed-with, in certain cases, some of them

---

* Shadows of Parliaments. *Umbra regis,* shadow of a king, is the vigorous expression which Tacitus puts in the mouth of Cæsennius Pætus.—[*Ann., xv., 6.*

offenses of a grave character; and in such cases the stipendiary magistrate is empowered to try the alleged offender in a summary manner.   At first blush, this seems almost like Oriental procedure; but we should learn not to judge of things too hastily.   The expression: Trying a man for murder before a justice of the peace and six jurymen, does sound ridiculous, indeed; and the idea of a justice of the peace (for the term " stipendiary magistrate " is unknown to us) trying a poor devil summarily for horse-stealing, embezzlement or felonious assault is shocking to us who have been trained from childhood to revere the jury system, and speak of it as the " palladium of liberty," " the birth-right of freemen," and-so-forth. Yet, as Judge Taylor, of the Queen's Bench of Manitoba, wisely said:

"Of this argument against any change being made in rights and privileges secured by old charters and statutes, a great deal too much may be made."*

It should be remembered, that the stipendiary magistrate of the North-West Territories is not the justice of the peace with whom we are familiar—that is, the man who keeps a dog-eared copy of the *Revised Statutes*, and holds court in the back part of his harness shop.   The stipendiary magistrate must be a barrister-at-law, or an advocate of five-years' standing.

But the jury reduced to six is surely a terribly dangerous innovation.   Is it not?   There is, in the minds of the best of men, a lurking, occult superstition as regards certain figures. Three, seven and twelve, and their multiples are mysterious numbers.   The labourer in the hay-field is stung by a bumble-bee; and he catches up three separate weeds or grasses, and rubs them upon the injured part.   It is practically almost impossible to select three herbs without finding one containing alkali.   The alkali neutralizes the acid from the bee.   Had a chemist selected one of the three, the one which contained the alkali, the result would have been ditto.   To the unlet-

---

* Queen against Riel, Manitoba Law Reports, Vol. II., No. 11, page 331.

tered rustic, however, the mystic number is the all-powerful, indispensible requisite. So of the number twelve; there were twelve tribes of Israel, twelve apostles, twelve tables, and there are twelve months in the year, and twelve signs of the Zodiac. As the origin of the jury system is lost in the obscurity of the Middle Ages, it is impossible to give any reason why the particular number twelve was fixed upon, aside from the fact of magic in the figures. If a large number of men are more certain to arrive at a correct conclusion than a small number, why not make it one hundred, instead of twelve?

One thing is certain: lynch law is almost, or quite, unknown in the North-West Territories. This is not our experience in the States. A friend* once remarked, in substance, that a crowd of regulators would seize upon a poor wretch, torture him into accusing himself of a crime, and hang him upon this confession, when if a rescue had been accomplished, and a jury selected from the same crowd, they would have listened to the vapourings of some pettifogger; and closed the farce by acquitting the defendant. Talk with any member of a band of regulators, and he will plead, in justification, the law's delay. Better summary justice to the guilty, than a farcical acquittal, or,

> "That worst of tyrants, an usurping crowd."

Any western lawyer with experience in criminal practice knows, that in exercising peremptory challenges on behalf of his client, in a criminal case, he does not pay more attention to nationality than to some other things, which the free-masonry of the profession forbids mentioning. Thus is the ancient glory of being tried by one's peers departed. The author is not advocating the abolition of the jury system. Far from it! But, as Judge Taylor has said: *A great deal too much may be said of rights granted by old statutes and charters.*

---

* Milton McLaughlin, of West Point, Nebr.

Rome denied her dependencies provincial senates. But England grants to Canada a parliament with plenary powers of legislation. Rome extorted, by taxation, from her provinces the entire expense of her home government. England's principal colonies regulate their own revenue; and England supports her home government. Rome laboured to destroy political unity in her provinces; Great Britain makes a federal republic in all but name for her North American dependencies. Rome had a privileged class who could appeal unto Cæsar; that class were the Quirites. England's colonies contain a like privileged class; but in the latter case it is not the Anglican Quirites, so to speak; but it is, rather, men charged with capital crimes. The exceptional outrages of which England and Englishmen have been guilty, were, in Roman provinces, not the exception but the rule.

Formerly all that portion of British North America bounded by the United States and Canada West (Ontario) on the South; by Canada East (Quebec) and Labrador on the East; by Hudson Strait and the Arctic Ocean on the North; and by Russian America and the Pacific Ocean on the West, was under the dominion of the Hudson Bay Company, a corporation existing by virtue of a royal charter from Charles II. of England, in the year 1670, to Prince Rupert, the hare-brained madcap who lost the battle of Marston Moor, as first president of the Hudson Bay Company, and fourteen others and their successors. Under the title of "the governor and company of adventurers of England trading into Hudson Bay," there were granted to them, by such charter, the sole trade and commerce of all those seas, straits, bays, rivers, lakes, creeks and sounds, in whatsoever latitude they shall be, that lie within the entrance of the straits commonly called Hudson's straits, together with all the lands and territories upon the countries, coasts and confines of the sea, bays, lakes, rivers, creeks and sounds, aforesaid, not previously granted. This country was denominated Rupert's Land; and was so designated on the maps for two hundred years, as all of us who studied geography previous to the year of grace 1870, know full well. The company was, by the charter, invested with the ownership of the soil, and with governmental powers within the region designated.

Construed in the light of its terms, and with respect to previous grants, there were grave doubts as to the right of the company to all the territory named; but they claimed such right; and, as they grew rich and powerful, they asserted their claim successfully.

Westward of the territory originally named Rupert's Land was that portion of British North America embraced within the Arctic and Pacific slopes. This was called the Indian, and afterwards the North-West, Territory. In the year 1821 the North-West Company was merged in the Hudson Bay Company; and the government granted the latter a monopoly in this territory for twenty-one years. A new license was granted, for the same period, in 1838. This latter expired in 1859. But the company, paying no attention to that fact, continued to exercise the franchise, though possessing no special privilege in the premises. Such was the condition of things up to the series of events hereinafter related. The history of the Dominion can never be written without a large space is given to Thomas Douglas, fifth earl of Selkirk, whom Professor Bryce ranks with Baltimore and Penn as one of the great triumvirate of American colonists. This truly great man was born at the family seat, Saint Mary's Isle, a peninsula (formerly an island) at the mouth of the estuary of the Dee, which river empties into Solway Firth, in June, 1771. It was this family seat which was pillaged by John Paul Jones and his reckless followers during the American Revolution. Selkirk died in France, at the age of forty-nine years.

To give anything like a history of Lord Selkirk's settlement would require more space than can be devoted to so interesting an espisode. The task has, already, been ably performed by Professor Bryce, in his valuable work: *Manitoba: Its Infancy, Growth, and Present Condition.* For the present purpose, let it suffice to say, that, in the year 1811, Lord Selkirk, at his own expense, fitted out a colony of Highlanders from Sutherlandshire, with a slight reinforcement of Sligo Irish, who were landed at York Factory, on the coast of Hudson Bay, at the mouth of Nelson River; and, during the spring following, were settled in the valley of the Red River of the North. Here the name of their gracious patron has been preserved in the nomenclature of the region.

The narrative of this little colony's life is one of the saddest chapters in the history of the world. In 1816 the massacre of Keldonan—most foul, fit to be named with Glencoe and Fort Pillow, differing only in degree from the bloody crime of Saint Bartholomew—was perpetrated, the victims being most innocent. From the relation of this tale, so revolting to every lover of his kind, the author begs to be excused.

About ten years thereafter came, successively, the triple plagues of the Rocky Mountain locust; the mice (scarcely less destructive), and the terrible deluge of 1827. During the winter of 1826 and 1827 the inhabitants of this region suffered beyond measure.

One of the most affecting incidents to which the author's attention has ever been called is related by the historians of that time. A woman was found dead with an infant on her back within a quarter of a mile of Pembina. "The poor creature must have travelled at least 125 miles in three days and three nights." As we think of this heroic mother goaded with the hope of succor, toiling through cold and darkness, now sinking in despair, now roused by the pleading of her little one to a renewal of the unequal struggle for life, anon uttering words of cheer and promises of help to her darling baby, as she pursues her course with the energy born of despair, and, at last, sinking down to die in sight of the haven she sought, what husband and father of us can think of it with dry eyes?

Leaving history here, let us pass to biography.

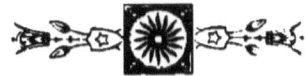

THE BLOOD OF ABEL.

PART THE SECOND.

CIVIS ANGLICANUS ERAT.

LOUIS RIEL.

THE BLOOD OF ABEL.

PART THE SECOND.

REBEL RIEL.

> " In men whom men condemn as ill
> I find so much of goodness still,
> In men whom men pronounce divine
> I find so much of sin and blot,
> I hesitate to draw a line
> Between the two, where God has not."
>
> —[*Joaquin Miller.*

LOUIS RIEL* was born October 22, 1844,† at Saint Boniface, Rupert's Land, on the western bank of a small creek which runs into the Red River from the East, a little North the site of the present city of Winnipeg. This stream is called after that historic river the Seine. The subject of this sketch was the son of Louis Riel, senior, and Julie de Lagimaudiere.‡ The house in which the child was born was a small, one-story, straw-thatched, log structure, containing but a single room. A saw-mill now stands about three rods North the historic spot. Louis was the eldest of eleven children, five of whom, with the mother, survive him.

Louis Riel belonged to the " Metis" or half-breed race. He was what they call in northern New England a French-Indian.

---

* Pronounced as though spelled Re-yell, with the accent on the last syllable.

† The Annual Cyclopedia for 1885, obituary " Riel," states that Louis Riel was born 1847. This shows of what stuff cyclopedias are made.

‡ Variously spelled.

Riel once told a gentleman in New York, that he had traced his ancestors from Sweden, successively, to Germany, France, Ireland, and, finally, to Canada. The name, he said, was originally spelled Riegal. He was the authority for the statement, that the Scandinavian form of the name was the patronymic Rielson.*

Louis Riel, junior, was the fifth in descent from John Baptist Reckhill, (for so the name was Hibernized†), a native of Limerick, Ireland, who migrated to Canada in the last decade of the seventeenth century ; and settled in what is now the province of Quebec. In the year 1705 this John Baptist Reckhill, or Riel, at Ile Dupas, diocese of Montreal, married Louise Cotta, aged twenty years, daughter of Francis Cotta and Joan Verdon. Six sons were the fruit of this union, and they all bore the surname of L'Irelande. The eldest received his father's name Frenchified, and was known as Jean Baptiste Riel De L'Irelande. He was baptized at Ile Dupas in 1705. One hundred and five years thereafter his grandson, bearing the same name, minus the De L'Irelande, left the parish of Bertheir for the North-West. Here he married a half-breed woman; and, in the year 1817, they had a son born and baptized at Crossing Island, in the south branch of the Saskatchewan, within the limits of the present district bearing that name, and near the seat of the late Half-breed War. This child was named Louis, and was the father of the Riel of history.

Louis Riel, the elder, was a man of ability and enterprise. He built the first grist-mill, driven by water, in the North-West. The history of this achievement is remarkable. The streams of Manitoba were all either too large or too small for the purpose. The Red and Assinniboine came under the first head. All the tiny creeks tributary to these were to be classed under the second. What was to be done? Farquhar called Necessity the mother of Invention; and his words have

---

* Riel's speech objecting to the sentence. See the Blue Book.

† A word coined by the author.

crystallized into a proverb. The Seine emptied into the Red River at Saint Boniface, and running parallel with it, or nearly so, was another tributary of the Red called Graisse Creek. The indefatigable half-breed conceived the idea of connecting these two little streams—absorbing the Graisse in the Seine, and, thereby, augmenting its force to a mill-driving capacity. In order to accomplish this it was necessary to cut a channel nine miles long. Considering the knowledge of engineering required; the limited means at command, and the uncivilized state of the country, this achievement was wonderful. Cyrus diverted the waters of the great river Euphrates into an artificial lake by a similar devise. He did it for the purpose of sacking a city, and slaying its inhabitants. The simple half-breed sought to give bread to the eater. The name of the general is immortal; that of the miller is forgotten. But so it will ever be as long as mankind honour the destroyer of a kingdom above the benefactor of a community, and the incendiary more than the architect. As a jurist Napoleon deserves to rank with Justinian; but the *Code* Napoleon stands in the shadow beside Marengo, Jena and Austerlitz.

So even in the case of so humble man as the elder Riel. It was as an agitator and partisan leader that he was chiefly famous. The reader of the first part of this volume will recollect the absorption of the North-West Company by the Hudson Bay Company. The first of these was organized in Montreal, and was essentially a French institution. The French half-breeds were linked to it by ties of race and language. On the other hand, after the union, the dominant company, which had Scotch officers and was totally Scotch, was disliked by the French-Indians. They chafed under its rule. It was an unkind, domineering step-father. The extent of its jurisdiction was doubtful, but its assumptions were great. It was the child of favouritism. The very charter to which it traced its existence, was the gift of an ignorant and profligate king, to a cousin who must be provided-for. The forced

construction put by the company upon its charter involved
the right to lands in which the Merry Monarch had about
the same title as had the Devil in kingdoms offered to Jesus
Christ.   The Hudson Bay Company was a giant monopoly.
It monopolized everything, even the commerce of the country.   The half-breeds were free-traders.   The American
frontier was too near, and the opportunity for gain too great
to allow of any restrictions.   In 1844 the company issued an
order threatening to refuse transportation, in its boats, of the
goods of any person trading on his own account.   On the
20th day of December, 1844, when the infant Louis lacked
two days of being two months old, the company assumed the
surveillance of the mails, and the right of searching the house
of any person suspected of trading on his own account.   The
French half-breeds refused to submit.   The Imperial Government was invoked; and, in 1846 four hundred soldiers
were sent to Fort Garry, the company's post at the confluence of the Assinniboine and Red Rivers, to preserve the
peace.

The year 1848 was the jubilee of political agitators. Philo-
sophical revolutionists, like Mazzini; patriotic rebels, like
Kossuth; political iconoclasts, like Bakounine sprang up, of
one accord, all over Europe, like the armed men, after the
sowing of the teeth in the classic tale.   The Pope fled, a fugitive, to Gaeta.   Louis Philippe's throne crumbled and fell.
The truth of Shakspere's words :
    " Uneasy lies the head that wears a crown,"
came home to the heart of every monarch of Europe.   Victoria was no exception.   In this year, of terrible experiences,
all but sixty of the troops at Fort Garry were recalled.

In the year 1849 William Sayer, a French half-breed, was
arrested, and lodged in jail, for trading on his own account.
Three others were arrested shortly afterwards, but were released on bail.   The elder Riel summoned his race to form a
vigilance committee, for their protection against the company.

This was done. Sayer was to be brought to trial on May the seventeeth, Ascension Day. On that day the half-breeds attended mass, at the cathedral in Saint Boniface; and then fifty of them crossed the river to Fort Garry. They were organized; and ready for fight, if necessary. Major Caldwell, acting governor of the company, was officiating magistrate, assisted by one Thorn, an Englishman, imported by Lord Durham, for the purpose of being employed by the company. Before such a tribunal the defendant had small show. Major Caldwell graciously informed the half-breeds, that a committee of them would be allowed to assist Sayer in his defence. In response to this invitation Riel entered the court-room, with twenty of his followers, armed to the teeth, and prepared to render the most substantial assistance. The main body remained outside. The prosecution closed their case, when Riel sprang to his feet; and declared Sayer acquitted. A loud yell from the half-breeds, within and without, greeted this announcement. In vain the magistrates protested, and asserted their authority. They could not cope with the rebels. Riel compelled the company to restore to Sayer the goods taken from him; to compensate him for his loss, and trouble; and to proclaim free-trade throughout the colony, and Louis Riel, senior, and his swarthy band, had to thank the political fire-eaters of Europe, who made it necessary to recall the troops, in 1848. From the hour of his triumph to the day of his death the elder Riel was the champion of his race. Financially his life was a comparative failure.

He died in 1864; and his body rests in the Catholic cemetery in Saint Boniface. No bard has sung the praises of this remarkable man. But, during the long winter evenings, many an aged half-breed makes the night less long with the story of his exploits in defence of his despised clan. Near his last resting-place the passing traveller might pause and fittingly repeat those beautiful lines from Gray's Elegy, too often quoted to need repetition here.

It is not intended to write anything which may be called a life of the younger Riel, a sketch is all that will be attempted. The author believes, that, before the reader closes this book, its object will sufficiently appear; and a simple sketch is all that is necessary.

Louis Riel remained at Saint Boniface, from the date of his birth until the year 1858; and it was here he received the rudiments of his education.

In narrating the life of a historic personage, cute anecdotes are always in order; and woe be to the sacrilegious iconoclast who dares to declare them apocryphal. George Washington's cherry tree, and Robespierre's wet stockings will always be associated, the one with the name of the best, the other with that of the worst of men. Tell, man or myth, shot the apple from the head of his child. It is a pretty story; and, as with the nursery-tale of Santa Claus, we look back with regret to the first time we heard, that it was untrue. We have no love for the person who told us this piece of bad news; and associate him with the man who first announced to us the death of a dear friend.

The life of Louis Riel, if it is ever written, will not be wanting in these little anecdotes.

It is related of him, that, at school, he was aggravated by another boy who wanted to fight him, when he said : "You want to fight, do you? Well, I will go and ask my father, and if he tells me to fight, I will meet you." It would be well, if every boy would adopt the same rule, providing always, that each one had as good a father as had Louis Riel.

The elder Riel was far above his position in life. He desired to give his eldest son a liberal education. But his means would not allow it. Dame Fortune, however, raised up a friend, in the person of the Right Reverend Bishop Alexander Tache, the present archbishop of St. Boniface. This eminent prelate, and distinguished scholar found a patron for the boy, Madame Masson of Terebone, at whose expense he was, in the year 1858, sent to the Jesuits' college, at Montreal, where he remained seven years—until the spring of 1865. Here he completed his classical course. It is to be presumed that his school life was that of most students.

One affecting incident is related of him. He had a class-mate for whom he contracted a lasting affection. The attachment was mutual. It was like the friendship of Damon and Pythias; even as the love of David and Jonathan, amiable above the love of woman. His friend was stricken down of small-pox. The attack was sudden; and the form malignant. Louis refused to leave him; and could not be driven or torn from his side. He remained faithful to the last. Before death the poor youth awoke from his delirium; and bade his faithful watcher a last farewell.

Whatever may be said of some incidents to be hereinafter related, one loves to turn from their contemplation to this affecting incident in the school-boy life of Louis Riel.

After finishing his college course, Riel remained one year in Montreal, when he went to Saint Paul, Minnesota, where he was, for a time, engaged as a clerk in a store. Archbishop Tache, in a letter to the author, thus briefly epitomizes the tale of his life for the next three years:

" He tried in the West all sorts of business, and failed to secure any success. In 1868 he came back to his native land, and remained with his family until the trouble of 1869."

Here we may be said to have passed the preliminary part of this little volume; and to have reached that portion of our work which bears less remotely upon the object of this book. Now, reader, let us have a perfect understanding, at the threshold. No justification of Louis Riel will be attempted. If his conduct is to be condemned, the author will leave that condemnation to the reader. For the purposes of this volume, it will be necessary to give a brief sketch of his public career which began in 1869. In giving such a sketch inci-dental comment can hardly be avoided. But the author begs the reader to consider any opinions unwittingly betrayed by such comments as what the lawyers call *obiter dicta*, not binding upon the judgment or conscience of anyone, save the author.

In the year 1867 the parliament of Great Britain passed what is known as the British North-American Act. This statute received the royal assent on the first day of July. By this act authority was given to create the province of Manitoba. It was shortly after this, that Fate, that stern arbiter of men and nations, forced a transfer of Rupert's Land, by the Hudson Bay Company, through the Imperial government, to the Dominion of Canada. To borrow a figure from Macaulay, the Hudson Bay Company had been to the North-West Territories what leading-strings are to a child. But, at this era, the child had out-grown the auxiliary. Like a selfish parent, who can not realize the growth of its offspring, the company tried to continue its control past its child's freedom day.

It is said that Chinamen have a way of dwarfing a pine tree till it will grow inside a flower-pot. It was a similar process which was tried in the North-West by the Hudson Bay Company. But, unlike the case of the Chinamen and the pine tree, it failed. It was Dame Partington vainly battling with Atlantic Ocean. *

The mania for mendacity seemed to seize every member and employee of the company like a contagion. Even good men, like Sir George Simpson, represented the country as unsuited for agriculture; and fit only for trappers and fur-traders.

By the surrender of its governmental powers the company got rid of an ugly question, involving the extent of its jurisdiction. The question was pushing itself into the arena and demanding a solution.

---

* Since writing the above I have learned for the first time, that Mercer Adam employs the same hackneyed figure.

By the terms of the transfer the company released all governmental jurisdiction over the territory; and all proprietary interest in the soil, excepting certain reservations made.

In the latter part of 1869 a formal deed was executed by the Hudson Bay Company, ceding this vast territory, over 2,300,000 square miles in extent, in consideration of less than $1,500,000 of American money. The grantors reserved all stations and trading-posts in actual possession at the time of the transfer. There is, in this country, a tract termed the Fertile Belt. This belt contains over three hundred millions acres. The company withheld the title to only one-twentieth of these lands, the reservation to be specified when the lands were surveyed and blocked-out for settlement. The deed also provided that all land titles conferred by the company up to May 8th, 1869, should be confirmed; and that the Indian claim, or title, should be liquidated or extinguished by the purchasers. Considering all this in comparison with the magnitude of the grantor's claim, it looks like a small price. But, viewed as a matter of legal right, or even substantial justice, the affair has a different appearance.

In regard to this transfer, the people of the purchased territory were not consulted. They were naturally anxious in regard to the situation.

At the session of the Dominion Parliament held for 1869, in Ottawa, an act was passed providing a provisional government for the acquired territory.

The Dominion act provided, that the colony should be governed by a Lieutenant-Governor and Council in which the people of the province had no choice.

In October of that year, Honourable William Macdougall was appointed the first Lieutenant-Governor.

Previous to this, Colonel Dennis had been sent out by the Dominion Government to superintend the survey of the lands in Assinniboia.* Now the half-breeds claimed a certain interest in the lands which were at the time of Colonel Dennis' visit, not transferred. The reasoning, in support of their claim, was not bad. The Indian right in the soil, was something which had always been recognized by both Great Britain and the United States. Courts might call that right by whatever name they saw fit; but its existence had always been recognized as a legal entity which was the subject of purchase. Upon racial grounds their right in the soil was something derived from their swarthy mothers. Then, too, the new-fangled survey would seriously disturb old land-marks. The French half-breeds in laying out their lands, had followed the method so familiar to anyone who has been in the Province of Quebec. Each man's piece had been laid out in a long, tongue-like strip, with a narrow frontage, whether upon street or river. The reason for this was two-fold. It was the social nature of the Celt, combined with the gregarious or tribal proclivities of the aborigines, developing in a desire to be near their neighbors. Furthermore the newness of the country required that the settlers be as near together as possible for mutual protection.

Everyone, even Lord Macaulay's school-boy, if he is alive, has read the story of Louis Riel placing his foot upon the surveyor's chain, and ordering him to desist. Authentic or otherwise, it is one of those dramatic little incidents, like Pizarro drawing the line in the sand, or Cato dropping the figs from the fold of his toga, which if not believed will always be told,

> "To point a moral, or adorn a tale."

It was not, however, Louis Riel who caused the uprising in 1869. That uprising was spontaneous.

The author is not writing history, therefore only a brief summary of facts will be given. Upon the approach of Honourable William Macdougall, appointed Lieutenant-Governor

* A district corresponding nearly with the present Manitoba.

of Assinniboia, the French half-breeds formed a committee, with John Bruce as President; and Louis Riel as Secretary. Riel was the real leader, and this position was forced upon him by virtue of daddyism. The purpose of the half-breeds was to prevent the entry of the Lieutenant-Governor into the country, until some guarantee could be obtained, that the rights of the settlers would be respected.

It will be borne in mind, that the charter rights of the Hudson Bay Company were franchises, or parts of the royal prerogative, granted to the company; that, as such, they had to be handed back to the crown to enable the latter to transfer them to the Dominion. The Canadian government, therefore, agreed to pay the purchase money; and the Imperial government became security for the amount. The day fixed for the final transfer was the first of December, 1869. As will be seen, when Governor Macdougall arrived at Pembina, in October of that year, he was preceding his authority by several weeks. The insurgents, who then numbered less than John Brown's raiders, at Harper's Ferry, built a barrier across the road which led from Pembina to Fort Garry and the then village of Winnipeg. The doughty Governor stopped at the frontier, like a drunken husband met at the threshold of his domicile, by his vixen spouse who forbids him the house until he comes home sober. He alternately domineered, raved, whined and begged. He extemporized a royal proclamation which excited contempt when the fraud was discovered. He appointed Colonel Dennis his deputy, who, if possible, made a bigger ass of himself than his principal. Then the Governor grew conciliatory, and wrote Riel a letter, which was condescension itself. Finally, meeting nothing but rebuff, Macdougall threw up his commission; and returned to Ottawa a disgraced and humiliated man.

While this gubernatorial aspirant was knocking at the door of his inhospitable province, the province itself was undergoing a radical change. In times of political revolution

events crowd each other in rapid succession. On the 2nd day
of November the insurgents seized upon Fort Garry, the company's post, at the junction of the Assinniboine and Red Rivers.
On the twenty-fourth day of that month a provisional government was organized with Bruce as President and Riel as Secretary. The President afterwards resigned in favour of Riel.
The original design was to have a council of twenty-four
members, twelve French; and twelve English. On the 8th day
of December, the date of the convening of the Vatican Council, a declaration similar in verbiage and sentiment to the historic document bearing date July 4th, 1776, save in its abjuration of allegiance, was issued by the new government. This
action alienated the English-speaking people, who were never
afterwards fully reconciled.

Wearisome details are not germane. Only a few salient
points will be touched upon.

On the 22nd of December, Riel seized and opened the
Hudson Bay Company's safe; and appropriated its contents,
amounting to a large sum in cash. This proceeding has been
denounced as an act of robbery. But Riel's conduct, in this
affair, will compare favourably with the conduct of John
Brown at Harper's Ferry. A party of Brown's men, led by
Alexander D. Stevens, demanded and took Colonel Washington's watch. After his capture, Brown was questioned in
regard to this affair, and stated, in terms, that he intended to
freely appropriate the property of slave-holders, to carry out
his purpose; but that to enrich himself by plunder was not his
object. Riel evidently had a like purpose. He intended
to make restitution, or force the Dominion to do the like, as
a condition precedent to reconciliation. For he attempted first
to negotiate a loan with the company. When refused this,
he resorted to force. When he took the money a memoran-
dum was left with MacTavish, the company's accountant. No
one believes John Brown to have been a robber; neither was
Louis Riel.

Early in the rebellion, Riel had captured Dr. Schultz and forty-four other English speaking colonists. Most of these were released through the humane efforts of a Miss MacVicar. But Schultz escaped. There is little doubt, but that this scoundrel, through one Shawman, *alias* George Racette, a reprobate half-breed, tried to bring upon the settlement the horrors of an Indian war. Be this as it may, he was largely responsible for all the trouble in Rupert's Land. He deserved death; but escaped it. But, on the seventeeth of February a far more important capture was made. Major Boulton and forty-seven men were taken prisoners. These were of the English or Canadian party, who were in arms against the provisional government. The commander was tried; and condemned to die; but subsequently pardoned.

Ten days prior to this capture Riel had been elected President of the new provisional government, with Thomas Bunn, Secretary of State; William B. O'Donoghue, Secretary of Treasury, and Ambrose Lepine, as Adjutant-General. Yet at no time, before or after the capture, did the insurgents renounce their allegiance to the Queen, or profess anything but loyalty and affection for their sovereign. They occupied a position similar to that occupied by the colonies at the time of the battles of Lexington and Bunker Hill. Certainly, if Samuel Adams and John Hancock were patriots, Louis Riel and William B. O'Donoghue might claim the name. Up to this stage there is much to commend and little to condemn in the conduct of Riel and his followers. They had seized the company's property, but they were forced to do this. War can not be maintained without finances. The insurgents had kept a strict account of all property so taken. If they compromised with the Dominion, it was their intent to make the government reimburse the company. Though the conduct of Riel and his followers had sometimes been warped by necessity, and strained by the force of circumstances, yet it was in the main to be excused, and even to be justified. But

4

for what follows, the leaders of the Half-breed Revolt might
rank with Bolivar and Sucre. Would to God, and for their
sakes, that the record might stop here! But the truth must
be told. Alas! there is now to be related an event which has
become sadly historical, and historically sad.

Among the prisoners captured with Major Boulton was a
surveyor, who had been sent out by the Dominion government,
named Thomas Scott, an Ontario Orangeman. This man, like
many public characters, was sentimentally one thing and historically another. He has served his purpose, as the hero of
more than one dime novel. Scott has been painted as a modern Leander—the embodiment of chivalry and devotion. It
has been written that Riel loved Scott's Hero, and hence what
will be related anon. But it is not only with the novelist that
Thomas Scott has been a favourite, but with the so-called historian, that is to say, the chronicler of the Genus Froude.
Mercer Adam says:

"Thomas Scott, a young English-speaking Canadian, it seems had become
obnoxious to Riel in the colony, by his somewhat effusive loyalty and a rather
reckless disregard of his own life. As an Orangeman, the Fenian flag on Fort
Garry, to this sturdy Briton, was a hated symbol of disloyalty and an irritating
emblem of rebellion. Scott's blood boiled at the sight of the flaunting flag, and he
became a bitter and out-spoken foe of the Catholic usurpers of the government.
Captured once by Riel, he refused to acknowledge his authority, and, escaping,
defied it. Captured a second time, Riel found him confirmed in his contumacy,
and he determined to reek his spite upon him. He ordered a court-martial of
his own choosing, to try his victim, but took care to hear no defence, to allow
him no counsel, and to keep him in ignorance of the crime of which he was accused. He did not even know the language and purport of the proceedings
that were taken against him. The mock trial occured on the evening of the 3d
of March, 1870, and lasted a little over two hours. Its finding was fatal; Scott
was sentenced to be shot at ten o'clock the next morning."

"The sentence fell on the incredulous ears of Riel's victim, but was impressed* by the grim humanity of the offer to send for a clergyman. On the
fatal morning, the clergyman—the Rev. George Young—secured two hours'
respite for the condemned loyalist, so as to obtain time to summon those who
would intercede for Scott's life, or if unsuccessful, to prepare the unfortunate

* According to Adam's syntax, the sentence received the impression.

for death. No intercession availed; Riel's black heart was obdurate; and his victim's death was too sweet revenge to forego it. At noon, in the court yard of Fort Garry, the revolting scene, the tragic horror, took place; Scott was in very truth shot down like a dog, and like a dog was buried."*

Professor Bryce says:

"With the object apparently of awing the other inhabitants into submission, a Canadian named Scott was barbarously shot by the Bois-brules, under the guise of a public execution."†

Rambaut, an American author, referring to Riel, says:

"At length he went so far as to order the shooting of a young Orangeman, Thomas Scott, against whom he had a personal grudge."‡

Alexander Begg comments on the affair as follows:

"Oh! shame on the spirit that prompted such an act! Was Mercy blind? Had Justice fallen asleep, and Wisdom turned her back upon the men who thus un-hesitatingly steeped their hands in blood?"§

Leaving fiery romance, and floral rhetoric, with a passing denial, let a few facts be related. Thomas Scott appears to have been a person of violent passions, and arbitrary temper. Like all of his order, he was filled with racial hate, and religious prejudice. He had once upon a time been fined, along with others, for an assault upon one Snow, their employer, from whom the assailants had extorted concessions, under threats of ducking. As the fine was paid, Scott expressed his regret, that they had not immersed Snow in the river. For then they would have got their money's worth. Scott had murdered a man named Parisien. He was one of the prisoners released at the request of Miss MacVicar, upon parol, that is upon his solemn oath, that he would not again take up arms against the provisional government. The caitiff had not only broken his parol, but he had aided Schultz in trying to incite the Swamp Indians to go upon the war-path. After his recapture, he was restive and furious, conducting himself more like a mad-dog than a rational and accountable being. Upon one occasion he took a board from the partition next his cell, with which he intended braining any person

* Pp. 205-6.   † Page 307.   ‡ Page 148.   § Page 301.

who should enter his prison. His fellow prisoners took this from him, yet his seditious conduct was acting upon the less prudent ones like a contagion. Under the direction of Riel and his council, Scott was tried by a drum-head court-martial; convicted and condemned. Ambrose Lepine, Riel's Adjutant-General, anxious to avoid blood-shed, offered to allow Scott to return to Ontario on condition of never afterwards setting foot within the Red River country. This offer was spurned, and Scott replied to proffered clemency with taunts of cowardice, as he chose to term the conduct of the chiefs in sparing the life of Major Boulton, a man of equal courage with Scott, and of far greater prudence. He told Lepine, in so many words, that the half-breeds dare not carry-out the sentence. He said, further, that if released the first use he would make of his liberty would be to kill President Riel. Finally, at the expiration of a brief respite granted for spiritual reasons, the unsubdued Orangeman was led out to his doom. Till the last moment he appears to have expected a reprieve. When the guards came for him he first realized his situation. The execution was under the personal direction of Lepine. Scott was made to kneel near the postern gate. A party of six men were his appointed executioners. The hardy Briton was less affected than many of his slayers, some of whom are said to have uncapped their guns before the order to fire was given. If Scott lacked all the other cardinal virtues, he certainly possessed that of fortitude. He fell pierced by several bullets, killed outright. Then the body was placed in a coffin and carried into the fort. It is claimed that even then he was still breathing, but this is a fiction. Afterwards the Protestant Bishop Mackray visited Riel, and begged the body, to give it Christian burial. For obvious reasons this was denied. These things gave rise to the belief that Scott was not killed, but only wounded; and led many to think that he would yet turn up alive. This was a delusion. The body of the unfortunate young man was consigned to an unknown grave. It was conjectured that the corpse was thrown into the river, but its resting-place will never be known till the sea gives up its dead, and the slayer and slain confront each other before the Searcher of All Hearts. If the reader desires to see this act of Riel condemned as "a mock execution," "a cold-blooded murder," and-so-forth, he can consult any work upon the subject in the English language. That Riel thought he was doing right, there is no doubt; but his opinion of the act is no defence. If honesty of purpose can be pleaded to justify an action intrinsically wrong, what condemnation is there for Torquemada or Leo the Isaurian? Saint Paul styles himself the chief of sinners; yet he says, that he conversed in all good conscience while persecuting Christians even unto foreign cities. When Thomas Paine was in the Luxembourg, in hourly expectation of death, he remembered with satisfaction that he had published an unclean libel on Christianity, which he had given to the world with an honest purpose. There can be no manner of doubt that Scott deserved a death more ignominious than a military execution—the doom of the gibbet. The author has been, and ever will be, an uncompromising foe of the jurisdiction of Judge Lynch. To murder a man because he has committed an infamous crime is but the compounding of felony. A government of doubtful jurisdiction should be chary of its authority. It may be argued that Riel's government was a lawful one, because the Hudson Bay Company in that region was a mere usurper; that the transfer of the franchise by the sovereign to the Dominion had not been accomplished when the Honourable William Macdougall entered the country; that, as the Queen, who was but the personification of legitimate sovereignty,* had failed to provide a lawful government for the people, the administrative "powers, incapable of annihilation," had reverted to the people for their exercise. So Riel, as a representative of the people, was not a rebel, not even a revolutionist.

* Guizot's History of Civilization.

But aside from that, it might be further said, that Riel had the legal authority to take Scott's life, under the God-given right of self-defence, the first law of nature; that if he allowed him to live, there was danger of mutiny, and of destruction to the provisional government; that if it was his right to establish such a government, it was his solemn and bounden duty to defend it when established. There is much force in this reasoning. The strongest argument against Riel's course with regard to Scott is based upon the plea of expediency. The shooting of Scott was like the beheading of Charles Stuart. The act itself was just, though, perhaps, illegal and possibly impolitic. Washington condemned Andre, and denied him even a soldier's death, dooming him to the halter. Scott had no counsel; neither had Andre. If, as Mercer Adam states, Scott was not informed of the crime with which he was charged, it was because he did not care to know its nature. If the trial was conducted in a strange tongue, it is no more than is happening every day, in the case of foreigners, without thought of any protest. Scott was given what Andre was denied; he was shot, like a soldier. Andre was hanged like a spy. The statement that Scott's body was consigned to an unknown grave, at first blush, seems cruel to his friends. But God did the same with the body of Moses, of whose sepulchre "no man knoweth until this present day." The reason for concealing his body, as before stated, is obvious. If the bones of Thomas Paine, ten years after death, caused such a rout as to justify the massacre of Peterloo, Riel was right in avoiding the occasion of an armed rising, by concealing the body of Scott. It is all the difference whose ox is gored. Britons denounced Washington as severely as they have Riel. Had the colonies been unsuccessful, Washington would have been a condemned traitor, instead of an immortal patriot. Then would historians have denounced the act of Washington, as they have that of Riel.

Joseph Riel, brother of Louis, in a letter to the writer,

under date of May 9, 1887, gives a full and comprehensive explanation of the causes which led to the death of Scott. The letter is in French. The following is a translation of a portion of it:

"Let anyone put himself in the place of those chiefs, and of the young man of 25 years, called by his nation to the presidency of a government at its most critical moment; let him consider all the circumstances; and the irritating opposition made to them; and he will be astonished, that they exercised so much clemency."

Never did British historians essay a more Sisyphean task than this same attempt to produce a martyr from the raw material of a hardened, a reckless though intrepid ruffian.

Riel complained, that, although he had obtained free institutions for Manitoba, he was forgotten as though he were dead. But for this one sad act, he would have lived an honoured life, the recognized champion of his despised race, and left a name scarcely second to William Tell. And yet his act was to be excused, if not justified, and would have met with universal approbation, but for the fact that Scott was an Orangeman.

If it is right, that the Muse of History should castigate Riel for his treatment of Scott, the muse should be impartial, just and equal in her chastisements. In the words of Macaulay:

"There should be one weight and one measure. Decimation is always an objectionable mode of punishment. It is the resource of judges too indolent and hasty to investigate facts, and to discriminate nicely between shades of guilt."*

For example, Louis Riel is condemned for the shooting of Thomas Scott, but let us instance a few other cases.

Alexander, misnamed the Great, ordered a hole to be made through the heels of Betis, under the tendon of Achilles; and a rope to be passed through the hole; and, with this rope tied to a chariot, he caused the brave general to be dragged around the walls of Gaza, until he was dead, for no other crime than loyalty to his sovereign. This royal madman afterwards boasted, that, in this affair, he had imitated Achil-

* Essay on Byron.

les, who treated Hector when dead, as he had treated Betis while living. This he-goat of Macedon, also caused Parmenio, the ablest, bravest, most faithful and most conservative of his generals to be butchered without the pretense of a trial; and without other testimony than a confession extorted, by the rack, from the craven lips of his recreant son. Alexander tortured a philosopher to death who had the courage to tell him the truth. In a drunken fit he stabbed to death his life-long friend, the brother of his own tender nurse. Concubinage, drunkenness, arson and sacrilege were among his lesser faults. The only good achievement of which he could claim the undivided glory was the taming of a wild horse. And yet this demoniacal wretch, beside whose cruelties the crimes of Nero and Robespierre pale into the insignificant, is pictured, by historians, as a divine hero, the pathfinder of Christianity, who paved the way for the Apostles.

Napoleon shot a Bourbon prince who approached his border; denied him counsel at his trial: and the consolations of religion in his last moments. Then with the phlegm of a a Thug, characterized the crime as *washing himself in the blood of a Bourbon.* Yet Napoleon found an apologist in a staid New England divine.

In the year 1842 Alexander Slidell Mackenzie, when in command of the brig Somers, had on board a stripling, of eighteen years, whose head had, probably, been turned by reading piratical romances. This boy related to a shipmate a cock-and-bull story about a conspiracy to kill the commander, to take the brig, and convert her into a pirate. The valorous captain did not deem himself safe until the boy Spencer, and two seamen, Cromwell and Small, were dangling at the yard-arm—condemned on about the same modicum of testimony, as suited the requirements of Mackenzie's royal namesake in the case of Parmenio and Philotas. Yet a court of inquiry, made up of distinguished naval commanders, with Old Ironsides, the grandfather and namesake of Charles

Stewart Parnell, as a member, exonerated Mackenzie. His government afterwards honoured him with an important command.

Lieutenant Alpheus W. Greely, of Arctic celebrity, ordered one of his men to be shot, perhaps justly, for eating too much dinner; and failed to make an official report of the shooting until it had already, become a matter of public notoriety. Yet his conduct in the affair has never been made a matter of judicial investigation. His statement, *ex-parte*, has been received as gospel truth. He has been *feted* by the world, and the present incumbent of the White House, has appointed him to a position scarcely second in importance to the post of cabinet minister.

Alexander, Napoleon, Mackenzie and Greely are heroes. But Riel is—what?

While the rebellion was in progress the Right Reverend Alexander Tache, Bishop of Saint Boniface, was at Rome, attending the Œcumenical Council, assembled in the Aula of the Vatican. A cablegram summoned the good pastor from the preparation of the short catechism, and the constitution *De Fide Catholica* to undertake a winter voyage, across the Atlantic. For upward of a half century this sublime and devoted man had laboured in the North-West. From an oblate of the Immaculate Conception, in 1843, he had risen to the episcopal dignity. His people knew him; and they loved him. Deserving and possessing the confidence, at once of his people, and of the Dominion Government, this noble prelate was, above all others, the man to quell the present unpleasantness. The politicians had failed. They turned their eyes toward Rome; and in the attitude of Ethiopia, beckoned the only man who could turn oil upon this troubled sea. The Bishop came. At once a true patriot, and a faithful shepherd, he knew that his people had wrongs. But true to that holy patriotism which the church inculcates, he had ever taught them, that the powers that are, are ordained of God. Render

to Cæsar the things that are Cæsar's. But cursed be he who
removeth his neighbour's land-marks. The Bishop came without any political commission in his pocket. Yet he brought
with him memoranda and letters of an official nature. There
was given to him by the Canadian government that unwrit-
ten authority most binding amongst men of honour. Such
as governs our presidential electors, and regulates love affairs
between people with honourable intentions. The arrival of
Bishop Tache in the settlement was a new era in the history
of this most awkward difficulty. On the 13th of March he
preached at Saint Boniface. The church was crowded. He
counseled moderation; assured his people of the good will of
the administration at Ottawa; said it was time for the Catholic and the Protestant to lay aside their religious differences
and work for the common good. The effect of this sermon,
and of a speech afterwards delivered before the council, was
like magic. Quiet was in a measure restored. Riel at once
released half of his prisoners, including Major Boulton. The
Bishop had, indeed, triumphed. He had paved the way for
the bloodless victory of Garnet Wolseley, that doughty hero
of many unfought battles. England has been, during the last
century and a half, distinguished for her cheap military heroes.
Indeed, she has not furnished a general of the first order of
merit since the days of Marlborough. The reader will remember that Wellington was an Irishman.

Garnet Joseph Wolseley was an Englishman, born near
Dublin, Ireland, June 4, 1833, to which place his family had
removed from Staffordshire. His father was a major in the
English army. The boy was educated at a private school.
At nineteen he entered the army with the rank of ensign. He
served in the Burmese and Crimean wars. In the latter he
was wounded and received a plaster in the shape of a badge
as knight of the Legion of Honour. He served during the
Sepoy Rebellion and the crusade to force opium upon China.
Whether or not this chivalrous knight ever tied sepoys to

the mouths of cannon and blew them into eternity, history
has failed to record. It is altogether likely that he did. Such
acts were done by the British, and their cruelty would be con-
sistent with Wolseley's career elsewhere. Then, too, he was
made a brevet lieutenant-colonel for his services during the
Sepoy Rebellion. He has received greater promotion for
services less meritorious. He was afterwards Deputy Quartermaster General in Canada, which post he held for several
years, being attached to the 90th Foot. When, at last, the
Macdonald Government resolved upon war, Garnet Wolseley
was selected to lead the British forces to the capture of Fort
Garry. In this campaign not a shot was fired. Yet the capture of any empty fort was sufficient to earn for Garnet J.
Wolseley the right to preface his name with "Sir." This valorous knight afterwards distinguished himself in the Ashan-
tee war, and against the Zulus. During the Nile expedition
to the Soudan, against El Mahdi, Wolseley signalized himself by cutting down palm trees, filling up wells ; and thus
destroying oases in that desert country. To charge him with
vandalism would be a libel upon Aleric and Albion. Sir
Garnet's greatest achievements have been against naked savages. It would be difficult to find a man more thoroughly
identified with every outrage which England has perpetrated
during the last thirty-five years, which is sufficient to make
his career during that period anything but an enviable one.
This competent military critic has seen fit to express himself in
very disparaging terms of the military career of General Grant.

Before entering the country Wolseley sent by a secret agent
a conciliatory proclamation to the people of Rupert's Land.
This document simply stated, in substance, that Her Majesty
had resolved to station some troops in the country. From its
terms it could not be considered a war measure in any sense
of the word. Riel himself assisted in the printing and cir-
culating of this proclamation; to show his loyalty he had
hoisted the Union Jack above Fort Garry. On the sugges-

tion of Sir George Etienne Cartier he was allowed to govern
the country from June 24, 1870, to the date of the occupation of Fort Garry by Garnet Wolseley. Whatever designs
others may have had, there can be no doubt but that throughout the entire difficulty Riel had remained steadfastly loyal
to his sovereign. He was actuated by the purest of motives.

Before the approach of the troops Archbishop Tache went
to Canada: for what purpose was left to conjecture. Some
said to obtain an amnesty for Riel, O'Donoghue and Lepine.
But when in the month of August England's goreless champion arrived, no amnesty was proclaimed. The trio remembering that the tender mercies of the wicked are cruel, refused
to trust the clemency of Sir John A. Macdonald. Wolseley
intended to come upon the Fort in the night-time, but a rain
prevented. He arrived the next day. As he entered the
fort at one door, Riel and his two comrades left at the other.
At one time the pursuer and pursued were only three hundred yards apart. A ferry crossed the Assinniboine by means
of a hawser; this was cut, probably by Riel, to prevent pursuit. Riel and his two companions crossed the Red River.
From the banks of Saint Boniface, the Sarsfield of the North-
West watched that capture of a garrisonless fort, which was
to lift the deputy quartermaster to be the first military hero
of a first-class war power. The quartermaster was elated with
his victory. What the feelings of the partisan chief were
can never be told. Boabdil looking down upon Granada from
the pass of the Alpuxarras would hardly furnish a parallel.
Both were fugitives, but Boabdil departed a broken and a
ruined man, while Riel, paradoxical as it may appear, fled a
victor from the scene of his triumph. The trio turned their
horses toward Pembina, whence Riel went to Saint Joseph.

The life of Louis Riel during the next fourteen years will
never be written. Its history would be more diversified than
the romance of Gil Blas, and hardly less entertaining. But
it is not the task which the author has essayed.

On the 2d of September, 1870, Archibald succeeded Macdougall, as Lieutenant-Governor. Though Archbishop Tache had pledged the honour of the administration for the amnesty of all offences, including the murder (?) of Scott, yet no amnesty was granted. In the year 1871 the Fenians were planning a raid upon the Dominion. They were in Pembina. Wherever Riel's sympathies may have been, he showed a firm purpose to keep faith with the government. Lieutenant-Governor Archibald called Riel from obscurity; and pledged him protection. The old leader came forward, like the regicide, in New England, during King Philip's War. He was the man, of all men, who had the ear of the French-speaking people of the province. Kosciusko was hardly more to the Poles of Napoleon's time, than was Louis Riel to the half-breeds of Manitoba. It was as though Andrew Jackson had risen from the dead, and was surrounded by the men who fought under him at Horseshoe Bend. Riel raised a body of two hundred and fifty men. The Lieutenant-Governor accepted Riel's services; and reviewed his troops. He even praised his loyalty. But how was that loyalty repaid? And how was the promise of protection kept? Hardly was the danger past when, in the early days of October, a reward of five thousand dollars was offered for the arrest of Riel. The promised amnesty was never proclaimed until April, 1875, and when it came it found Louis Riel an outlaw, so declared seven months before upon a judgment entered because of his failure to appear and answer an indictment which charged no offense whatever.*

In the year 1872, an election was about to take place. The administration were anxious to have Riel out of the country. In the month of February Archbishop Tache visited the ex-chief at Saint Vital; and tried to induce him to leave the country. Through the personal influence of the man to whom

---

* I refer the reader to Appendix B for the form of this indictment; and to Bouvier's Law Dictionary for an explanation of the meaning of "Outlawry."

he owed everything, Riel was induced to accept, as an indemnity, four hundred pounds—three hundred for himself, and one hundred for his family—and leave the country. This he did probably with about the same thought as Jugurtha left Rome. The money received by Riel, at this time, has been called corruption money. If so, it reflects as little credit on the donor as upon the receiver. But Riel's account of the affair, as well as his subsequent conduct, shows that he did not so regard it.

For more than a century American children have been taught to regard Paulding, Williams and Van Wart, the captors of Major Andre, as honest patriots. But there is more evidence of their corruption than there is against Riel.

Public opinion forced Riel's return from exile, and he was present at the election. He was a candidate for Parliament. His election was conceded. Sir George Etienne Cartier was beaten in Montreal, by one Jette. Riel was asked to stand back for Sir George to be returned for Provencher, as the district was called; and he did so. It was about this time, that Judge Dubo christened Riel "David;" and, afterwards, Riel used the name. The record of his naturalization bears the signature "Louis David Riel." This name was bestowed upon him because, like the second king of Israel, he hid himself away from those who sought his life.

Riel was thrice returned to Parliament. The first time in October, 1873, by acclamation. It was during this campaign (as we Americans would call it), that agents of Sir John A. Macdonald sought out the ex-chief skulking in the woods, awaiting his election to Parliament. Most politicians are cynics; and Sir John A. Macdonald was no exception. The great premier had a supreme confidence in, as he had a sovereign contempt for, the venality of mankind. Sir John's agents offered Riel $35,000 to leave the country for three years. They told him, further, if that was not enough, to state what he wanted. They offered to pay his expenses to Europe, or to any part of the world. But this man, whom his enemies have charged with being a venal mercenary, refused the offer.

Riel was returned again in January of the following year. At this time the feeling in Ottawa was intensely against him. The public furor was at fever heat, because of the shooting of Scott. He did not attempt to sit in Parliament. In the month of March he appeared suddenly and mysteriously in the clerk's room at Ottawa, signed the roll of membership, in that characteristic autograph, never to be mistaken; and then he vanished like an unsubstantial pageant of a vision.

On the 16th day of the following month he was expelled the House, by a vote of 124 to 68. Many, who voted " aye " on that memorable day, and even at other times urged the extradition of Riel from the United States, as a murderer, have since attempted to rebuild their party edifice, with the scaffold of Regina for the chief corner-stone. He was returned for the last time in September, 1874.

In the year 1875 Riel was banished for five years. During this time he resided nominally in the United States. In the year 1874 we hear of him at Woonsocket, Rhode Island, where he spent a week with an aunt. In the autumn of 1875 we find him in Washington, whither he had gone recommended to Major Edmund Mallet. A friend who saw him about this time, thus describes him in a letter to the author:

" Riel was, in every way, a perfect gentleman. He possessed talents for leadership found in but few men. He was born a liberator. William O'Brien now in Canada appears to me to be such a man as Riel was. He was one of those most polite men I ever knew. His conscience was as tender as a sister of charity's. . . . . The man was not of the world. He was like a monk in it; *except* that he was like a true knight when the question of the Metis people was involved. "

At the time Riel came to Washington he considered himself absolved from every obligation to the Dominion, that government having refused amnesty to Lepine, and violated other pledges. The object of his journey, and the then constant labour of this enthusiast, was to wrest Manitoba from the Dominion.

Excessive toil, bitter disappointment and galling poverty so wrought upon his sensitive nature that reason was dethroned. He had come to Washington with one thousand dollars, the donation of a wealthy Canadian. In the space of several months he had given this, piece-meal, to a blind Italian beggar who sat daily in front of the Presbyterian church on Ninth street. Thus was this high-minded and generous patriot reduced at once to madness and penury in a strange city. But God provided a friend. Riel was possessed of the delusion that he must die for the salvation of his race. Major Mallet took forcible possession of his person. But finding him moneyless, he was compelled to borrow cash from Father Keane, now Bishop of Richmond, to remove the unfortunate North. Riel remained for nineteen months at the Beauport lunatic asylum in the province of Quebec.

His ailment was megalomania. This word is not found in the dictionaries. It is derived from two Greek words, *megale*, great, and *mania*, madness. It is a most peculiar and deceptive form of insanity. Its victim might easily pass for a sane person amongst the unobservant. The person afflicted with this mental disorder imagines himself charged with some great mission and altogether a most important person.

Riel was incarcerated under the name of La Rochelle. He remained under the treatment of the medical superintendent, Doctor Francis Roy, until he had recovered. He was discharged from the asylum January 21, 1878. Doctor Ray found his case a most peculiar one, and one requiring careful treatment. To this gentleman Riel confessed his true name.

The American Annual Cyclopædia for 1885, insinuates, that Riel might have been confined at Beaupart for the purpose of concealment. Such an insinuation betrays the extreme stupidity and ignorance of the writer. Riel was placed in the asylum by the provisional government, upon the certificate of its examining physician. The laws there are very strict to prevent the incarceration of persons other than actual lunatics. Major Mallet of Washington, considered him insane at that time, from actual personal knowledge. The opinion of this intelligent Christian gentleman is worth that of one hundred of Sir John A. Macdonald's mercenary sycophants.

On the discharge of Riel from Beauport Ayslum he revisited Washington, and related his treatment, as an insane patient to his *alter ego*, Edmund Mallet. His second sojourn at the capital was less protracted. There can be little, if any, doubt, that his recovery was complete. In 1878 he appears as a farmer at Saint Joseph, Minnesota, where he remained about a year. In 1879 he removed to Montana. Here he married a half-breed girl named Marguerite Bellimense, by whom he had two children. The first of these, John, was born May 9, 1882, in a prairie home on the banks of the Missouri. This son, though " born in the United States and subject to the jurisdiction thereof," was the child of an alien. The father, with characteristic delicacy, had refused to become an American citizen while his term of banishment continued.

Afterwards he declared his intention to become an American citizen. In the month of March, 1883, he applied to the district court of the United States at Helena, Montana, and on the sixteenth day of that month he became a citizen. Levi Jerome and E. L. Merrill (full Christian name unknown) appeared as witnesses.

During the same year Riel removed to Saint Peter's Mission, abandoned trapping, by which he had gained a precarious livelihood, and settled down to school-teaching, under the direction of the Jesuit fathers. It was at this place that his little daughter, Mary Angelica, was born, September 17, 1883.

As the last part of this volume will be devoted to Riel, considered as an American citizen, perhaps there is no better time than the present at which to estimate the man in the abstract.

5

The usual method of weighing public characters is to adopt as a standard, or unit of measure, some person who has passed into history. Burton says that comparisons are odious. Benjamin F. Butler put it milder: " Analogies are ever false and illusory." A comparison drawn between different men is often ridiculous and too often disgusting.

For example, we have the strolling renegade, John Baptist Clootz, comparing himself to the great Scythian, Anacharsis, and even assuming his name. The assassin of Abraham Lincoln likened himself to William Tell. A certain would-be historian tried to compare the fiasco at Fort Garry to the surrender at Sedan, which occurred eight days later, and thought Garnet Wolseley a Von Moltke. There was once a man who could trace in Andrew Johnson a resemblance to Cato. The trustees of Washington College, Virginia, have linked the name of Robert E. Lee with one that is a synonym for purity, patriotism and justice throughout the world. This is about as appropriate as would be the coupling of the names of Absalom and Robert Bruce. When Horatio Seymour, a very respectable gentleman of no ordinary ability, was nominated for president of the United States, some newspaper correspondent compared him to Cicero. James Anthony Froude, the miserable apologist for England's misgovernment of Ireland, thought Julius Cæsar resembled Jesus Christ. This is the man who called Daniel O'Connell an empty demagogue.

Such comparisons have not been wanting in the case of Louis Riel. Why not? They serve to round-off a period. But truth, and not rhetoric, is the object of this little book. Riel has been compared to John Brown, to Rochejaquelein, to the Young Pretender, and to everybody else whom he did not resemble. Such analogies are the resort of oratorical historians who are too lazy to delineate character.

A friend says that Riel was Joan of Arc and Pontiac combined. This comparison is a nearer approach to justice than any it has been the author's good fortune to hear or to read.

The truth is, that every man has his separate individuality, and there is seldom any real resemblance between men of different nationalities or even separate families. Two distinct particles of matter can not fill the same space; two distinct characters can not act the same part in the drama of human history. Could we approach the Milky Way its stars would become distinct entities; the space between them would widen until what resembles now a fleecy cloud would be a vast system of worlds, or, perhaps, a myriad of systems, with almost inconceivable space between its rolling orbs. So, too, with individuals. We may see two men who appear to be alike in every particular. Inspect them more closely and the likeness departs. Alexander and Charles XII.; Cicero and Burke; Washington and Epaminondas; Clootz and Train, each and all, were men of distinctive individualities, resembling each other at a distance; but appearing unique in their personal characteristics upon a closer inspection.

Rochejaquelein and Charles Edward were, each of them, relics of a defunct royalty; while Riel was the champion of a despised race. Riel will, undoubtedly, fill a space in Canadian history similar to that of John Brown in American history. Yet Napoleon said that history it but a series of lies, agreed upon. John Brown was an illiterate man of few words, who, whatever may be said of his judgment, had not about him one scintilla of selfishness. Riel had received a classical education; was somewhat loquacious; and was actuated, in main, by the most generous of impulses.

The position which Riel is entitled-to in history; and his relations to the government under which he lived, resemble those of Ethan Allen. Both these men fought for the rights of settlers to their land; each contended against a horde of grasping land pirates who were fostered by England; whose entire law of tenantry is but a barbaric relic of feudalism; each was made a prisoner, and, too, while leading French Canadians against British soldiers. Each of these founded a provincial or state government, though not a nation. Riel contended for what was, not only a just claim, but a plain legal right. Allen fought for what was just, but he met with force and chastised "with twigs of the wilderness" officers, charged with the enforcement of the decree of a court. Both Allen and Riel were successful. But the latter died as a condemned traitor; the other has been justly honoured by having his bust placed in the old hall of representatives as one of two whom Vermont delighted to honour. Both Allen and Riel speculated with religion. Aside from Allen's peculiar religious views, and his outrageous profanity, there is little in his life which does not excite our enthusiastic admiration. Riel's private life was free from vices. For one public act he has been condemned. Unfortunate, indeed, is he who, at twenty-five years of age, rises from the position of a grocery clerk to be the all-but despotic ruler of his people. But fortunate does he become who, having thus risen, commits but one act of folly, great though that folly be.

The Encyclopædia Britannica, in its article, "Red River," devotes less than a dozen lines to Louis Riel and his life work. It runs as follows:

"At the transfer of territorial jurisdiction to the Canadian government in 1869 the Bois-Brules, under a certain Louis Riel, (son of a Frenchman who had built the first mill on the Red River), revolted and declared an independent republic.* Colonel (now Lord) Wolseley was despatched with a force of 1,400 men and without bloodshed took possession of Fort Garry on the 24th of August, 1870. The only striking feature of the expedition was the remarkable energy with which the difficulties of transportation were overcome. Riel in 1885 became the leader of another unsuccessful insurrection of half-breeds in the same region."

At first blush it would seem an easy task to write history. But experience shows the twelve labours of Hercules to be lighter. Look back at the foregoing account of Riel from the Encyclopædia. Then compare it with another account.

---

* Untrue, as the reader will remember. It is thus that Tory England, after choking a man to death, lies over his corpse.

There was once a man named Tacitus. He was a great man too. He wrote the history of the reign of an emperor called Nero. In his account of the fire in Rome which occurred during that reign, the historian, speaking of the Christians, says: " The author of that name was Christ, who, Tiberius, being emperor, by the Procurator Pontius Pilate, suffered death."* Thus, with a single dash of the pen, did the wisest man of his day and generation pass by a name which it would be blasphemy to compare with any name given under Heaven or among men. Tyrants can make laws; they can hang, and they can crucify, but the chroniclers who record their deeds can not make history.

---

* *Tacitus, Annal., XV., 44.* See, too, Carlyle's Essay on Voltaire.

THE BLOOD OF ABEL.

PART THE THIRD.

CITIZEN RIEL.

CIVIS AMERICANUS FUIT.

THE BLOOD OF ABEL.

PART THE THIRD.

CITIZEN RIEL.

" Is man like a vegetable, a fossil, that he must belong to a bed of loam, or marl, just as he happens to originate? " —[*Hugh Henry Brackenridge.*

SALLUST and Saint Luke have perpetuated two orations, the greatest of their kind. The one was spoken by a judge to his associates; the other by a prisoner, with chains on his hands. When the question of punishment, in the case of the Catilinian conspirators, was before the Roman Senate, Cæsar addressed that body. His speech on that occasion is, with the single exception of Paul's defence before Agrippa, the finest forensic argument on record. The great Roman began his address as follows:

" It behooves all men, O Conscript Fathers, who deliberate concerning doubtful matters, to be free from hatred, friendship, anger and pity."*

Thus doth it become one to be who would speak upon the case of Louis Riel.

This is no party pamphlet. The writer speaks as an American to Americans. On the 16th day of November of the year 1885, Louis Riel, an American citizen, was hanged at Regina, in the North-West Territories, within the Realm of Her Britannic Majesty, for high treason against the crown and dignity of the Queen of Great Britain and Ireland. The

* Sallustii Bellum Catilinarium, LI.

attention of President Cleveland and Secretary Bayard was called to the facts, but they refused to act in the matter. The Secretary of State did not consider the matter of sufficient importance to be mentioned in his annual report. Was this inaction of the United States government justified by the facts in the case? The solution of this problem is the subject before us.

For the purpose of this volume it boots little that Louis Riel was Catholic or Protestant; that he was of French or of Germanic, or of Indian, or of Irish, or of Swedish extraction; that he was patriot, fanatic, imposter or madman. For such purpose, it matters not whether he be considered a John Brown, a Count Cagliostro, an Anacharsis Clootz, a Don Quixote, a George Francis Train, or a William Tell. One proposition is beyond cavil: He was, at his death, an American citizen. That undisputed fact stamped upon him a dignity which neither race, religion, character or condition could obliterate. *Civis Americanus fuit.* Forget all beside.

Whether it be termed a freak of Nature, or one of her laws of which men talk much and know nothing, it is, in either event, a continuously recurring fact, that offspring do not partake in equal proportion, of father's and mother's characteristics. Though always resembling both, in a certain degree, the child will bear the likeness of one more than the other. Mulattoes show more strongly the peculiarities of either African or Caucasian; Zambos of Negro or Indian; and half-breed of Caucasian or aboriginal. There are few exceptions to this rule. So it may be regarded as a part of the law of Hereditary. Some of the half-breeds of the North-West, from their fair complexions, Celtic features and suave demeanor, might easily be mistaken for Frenchmen; while others have the physical and mental characteristics of their squaw mothers. Even the educated Indian, whatever his opportunities to embrace civilization, has, almost without exception, gravitated to the *tipi* and the breech-clout. Samson

Occom, the Whitfield of the forest, returned to the native savagery of his race, like a dog to his vomit.

After the revolution in Manitoba, there were many striking examples of this. The rebels had secured the concession of their demands. The government issued negotiable land-scrip. The Celtic half-breeds settled down, in their new province, to agriculture and quietude. But the nomadic ones, Esau-like, sold their scrip to speculators; and, finding themselves crowded by advancing civilization, moved to the wild West, and joined friends and relatives who had gone before in trapping the beaver and hunting the buffalo. Thus, upon the banks of the Saskatchewan, principally along its south branch, between its confluence with the northern and a point upon the southern branch, in line with the elbow in the north branch, there grew up a settlement of half-breeds who were, nearly all of them, immigrants from the country along the banks of the Red and Assinniboine.

In western America civilization makes gigantic strides in a few years. It would be hardly exaggeration to say, that the buffalo is as much a thing of the past as the mastodon. Trapper tales read like the story of Romulus and Remus. Most of the half-breeds in the Saskatchewan country accepted the inevitable. They settled down upon the land which, as it was remote from civilization, no one wanted. It is a strange but true paradox, that poverty is the father of property. There can be no property in air because there is plenty of it, equally distributed all over the world. It is a truism of the Common Law of England, that there can be no property in water. This is true simply because, that, wherever that law has prevailed, there has been plenty of water. But England's law of land-tenure and landed estates is the most complex part of her jurisprudence. Why is this? Because her territory is small and densely populated. Her people are land-hungry.

When the patriarchs inhabited Syria, land, except in the civilized portion, was worth nothing. Metes and bounds were unknown. The only recorded land purchase is the sale of the double cave as a burial-place for Sarah. But the servants of Isaac and Gerar strove for the possession of two wells.

So in the primitive days of the North-West, land was plenteous. To use the vernacular of the West, the half-breeds "squatted upon claims." They cleared away the forests, tore up stumps; removed the rocks; ploughed the earth, and made the desert to blossom like the rose. After they had built themselves homes in the wilderness, the coal-beds of the Saskatchewan were discovered to be profitable. Then came capital. The resources of the country, in forest, field and mine, began to develope. Thereupon came the land-sharks. The "squatter's" rights were disregarded. Syndicates and monopolists seized upon the lands. The settlers had followed the Quebec rule, in laying-out their claims. The merciless surveyor blocked-out the lands in sections.* By such a survey the division of every half-breed's claim was a physical certainty. If he got to the land office before any other man overreached him, he might secure one part of his farm; upon the whole of which he had worked, like a slave, for many years.

Put yourself in the half-breed's place. Imagine yourself ousted of your farm by the brainless spawn of an *effete* and emasculated aristocracy. The spade must give way to the eye-glass. We all know what English syndicates, composed of lords' bastards, have done in our own country, in the line of land robbery. We have had a press which has been free and loud in its utterances, especially in those quarters where such a course would secure the most votes. Yet, with due regard to exaggeration, it can not be denied, that English land-grabbing in the United States has been a burning shame. Yet we could write; we could speak; we had a president who respected the rights of a homestead-entryman, with a

* In the West, a section means a square mile.

ballot in his hand, more than he did—but the writer is antici-
pating.

Alas, for the poor half-breed! He could neither read nor
write. He petitioned; he prostrated himself at the feet of
Canada's great premier; but the government was deaf and
dumb. A writer in the Annual Cyclopæda for 1885 says:

"The people of the older provinces of Canada hardly knew that the half-
breeds had any grievances at all until the eve of the rebellion."

The language is worthy the asinine dolt who penned the
lines. Did not know! Why? Because petition upon petition
had found its grave in the pigeon-hole at the Interior Department to be resurrected only by the trumpet-blast of another
Gabriel.* Sir John A. Macdonald had not only no disposition to do justice; but he had not even the susceptibility of
the unjust judge, mentioned in the gospel. There is little
doubt, that Seneca lived and died in blissful ignorance of the
martyrdom, and, of the very existence of Saint Paul, although
he lived in the same city. That is no proof, that Paul was
not beheaded.

Hope deferred made the heart sick. The poor half-breeds
became discouraged. There were many in the Saskatchewan
settlement of Saint Laurent who participated in the uprising
of 1869. The recall of Riel was suggested and determined-
upon. All eyes were turned toward Montana. A committee of four half-breeds was sent to the Sun River country.
One of the committee was Gabriel Dumont, destined to figure
in the future history of the country. They journeyed for
seven hundred miles on Indian ponies. They found the ex-
chief at Saint Peter's Mission, about twenty miles from Sun
River, upon the banks of the Missouri. The messengers in-
vited their old chief to return and lead them in a constitutional
agitation for securing their rights. History contains few incidents more touching than the story of this pilgrimage.

* Gabriel Dumont was the commander and chief of Riel's army in the Saskatchewan Rebellion.

Time may brand it as apocryphal, as it already has the tale of Pocahontas and John Smith.

> " I've stood upon Achilles' tomb,
> And heard Troy doubted. Time will doubt of Rome."

Riel's friends at the Mission entreated him to remain in Montana. But he decided to go to the Saskatchewan. The wisdom of this choice will not be debated here. It may be argued that Riel was an American citizen and had renounced his allegiance to the Queen; his country was at peace with England; and, consequently, he had no right to interfere with England's colonial politics.

There was once a Frenchman named LaFayette. His country was at peace with England. He came across the water to interfere with England's colonial politics. There was a difference, however, in this: LaFayette brought his sword along, while Riel intended a peaceful agitation circumscribed by the constitution. But there were other differences: LaFayette was successful. In his old age, his visit to the land he befriended was the event of the year 1824. A mountain, the third in height east of the Rocky range, has been named in his honour. The story of Riel is but half told.

He arrived in the Saskatchewan country, in the summer of 1884. In company with others he began a constitutional agitation, which proved abortive. Seven months of this effected nothing but an increase of the mounted police, a body of men—half-civilian, half-soldier—acting as a constabulary force in the North-West Territories. They were organized in 1874; and ten years thereafter, at the time of which we write, they were increased to five hundred men. Thus did the poor children of the desert ask bread; and receive a stone. The council, presided over by Lieutenant-Governor Dowdney, had recommended their claims. But the great premier (for great he is) heard them not. Pharaoh's heart could not have been harder. Alas! he was soon to learn " how much the wretched dare." When the history—I mean not such brilliant party pamphlets, as Mercer Adam's really able work; when the *history* of the North-West rebellion is written, it will appear, that few people would have borne what the poor half-breeds endured.

If it was glorious to go to war over a three-penny tax upon tea, the half-breeds of the North-West were surely justified in fighting for their homes. For,

> "How can man die better
>   Than facing fearful odds,
> For the ashes of his fathers,
>   And the temples of his gods;
> And for the tender mother
>   Who dandled him to rest,
> And for the wife who nurses
>   His baby at her breast."

Riel had entered the country with the purest motives. Before he commenced his constitutional agitation, he visited the Mission, Saint-Laurent-Grandin; called upon Father Fourmond, who had in charge the missions of Saint Lawrence, Saint Anthony of Padua and the Sacred Heart. He asked the ecclesiastic for his blessing; and ever after attended strictly to his duties as a Catholic.

He has been charged with apostasy. The discussion of this question would be without the purpose of this volume. If Riel taught the doctrines ascribed to him, he was, nevertheless, quite as orthodox as the Nestorian, Prester John, whose strange career furnished the basis for so many pious legends; and whose uptopian kingdom was the object of so many pilgrimages. An indignant congregation left the church, when that unworthy pastor, Nestorius, declared the Blessed Virgin to be mother of Christ, but not of God. The verdict of Christendom was against Nestorius; and he was driven in disgrace, from his see. Seven centuries thereafter half of Christendom were almost ready to canonize the disciple of the great heresiarch. Verily do times change; and men change with them. The charges against Riel's orthodoxy have been made upon authority highly respectable. But again let Macaulay's recommendation of one weight and one measure be borne in mind.

On the 18th of March, 1885, the first coercive act was committed. Mr. Edward Blake, the liberal leader, in a speech delivered at Lindsay, in January, 1887, said:

"I have never denied, that there was treason on the banks of the Saskatchewan, amongst those half-civilized illiterate, misguided, but also much abused people. There was treason under the law." *

The author, presumptious as it may seem, will take issue with the liberal statesman, before the close. But, admitting the truth of his proposition, Louis Riel was guilty of treason under the law. Yes, just as Virginius was guilty of murder under the law.

On the date last named, the half-breeds at Batoche, having formed a provisional government, rose in a body, under the leadership of Riel and Dumont. Riel persistently denied being the leader. He claimed, that all were equal, and he signed himself " Louis David Riel, *Exovede.*" This word *exovede* was one of his own coinage. He derived it from the Latin *ex*, out of; and *ovile*, the sheep-fold. Thus signifying, that he was only one among the others. His etymology was unique, eccentric and far-fetched, to say the least. The exact number of Riel's following is a little uncertain. An estimate is all that can be given. This the author forbears to make. The Indian camp-followers of Riel were the uncertain element, as those desultory soldiers of fortune always are.

The nucleus of the half-breed settlement upon the Saskatchewan, was the village of Batoche, situate upon the south fork. One mile below Batoche, upon the same fork is Dumont's, or Gabriel's, Crossing, so called from the half-breed leader who kept a ferry there. The reader will remember, that Carleton lies fourteen miles from Batoche, upon the north branch. Prince Albert lies farther down the same branch.

---

* Toronto Weekly Globe, January 28, 1887 ; Speeches by Honourable Edward Blake, (Hunter, Rose & Co., Toronto), page 421.

Nearly the whole country settled by half-breeds of this settlement in 1885 would be embraced within the surface of a superficial isoseles triangle, whose base would be a line drawn from Carleton to a point a little south-east of Gabriel Dumont's Crossing, and whose apex would be at Prince Albert. The distance from Gabriel's Crossing to Prince Albert is twenty-five miles. The portion of this half-breed settlement around and near Batoche was called Saint Laurent. The whole number of half-breeds in the settlement in 1885 was less than five hundred, and the male adults capable of bearing arms numbered about seventy.

The little village of Batoche lay about half-way between Clarke's Crossing and the junction of the two forks, a little nearer the former. The greater part of the village was on the right bank. Here were the stores of Kerr Brothers and George Fisher. Upon the left bank were the stores of Walters and Baker. Riel, Dumont and their following to the number of about forty men, seized and looted the stores. An account was kept of the goods taken.

Shortly after this outbreak the half-breeds at Batoche were favoured by a visit from Thomas Mackay,* of Prince Albert. This man was a Scotch-Cree half-breed of considerable intelligence who had enrolled himself as a volunteer for the suppression of the revolt. Mackay thus described his mission. He said that he went to Batoche: "To see if I could point out to them [the half-breeds] the danger they were getting into in taking up arms. I knew a great many of them were ignorant and did not know what they were doing; and I thought I might induce them to disperse."†

It has ever been the policy of a conquering nation to select certain members of a subjected race as the recipients of her special bounty, hoping, through them, to keep mastery over their fellows. This was Roman state-craft, and England is

---

* Spelled also McKay.   † The Queen *vs.* Louis Riel, p. 17.

no stranger to the art. Thomas Mackay was one of those petted panders. While at Batoche he met Riel. During a conversation held with Mackay, Riel called him a speculator and told him his blood was frozen. In the heat of his passion he said many other things which he had better left unsaid. He felt and spoke much as did Arminius, the German liberator, to his brother Flavius, who followed the Roman standard to fight against his country, in that celebrated interview so graphically described by Tacitus.* The language of Arminius has been beautifully rendered by Praed in English verse, and would be a fair paraphrase of Riel's language on this occasion:

> " I curse him by the gifts the land
>   Hath won from him and Rome,
> The riving axe, the wasting brand,
>   Rent forest, blazing home."

While the fiery chief was speaking with so much emphasis and freedom, the wily and phlegmatic British spy was drinking-in his words, which would be reproduced in the court-room at Regina. The language of Riel upon the occasion, as testified to by Mackay, was judicially interpreted as the growl which accompanied the tiger's jump—what lawyers call a part of the *res gestæ*.

On the 22nd of March Sir John A. Macdonald, the premier, received a dispatch to the effect that Riel and a gang of his men, numbering forty in all, had seized the mail-bags at a way office near Duck Lake, and taken eight horses belonging to the mail-carrier; that they had plundered several stores; that they were encamped at Duck Lake, and were threatening Fort Carleton; that the wires were down between Prince Albert and Clarke's Crossing. The next day he informed the House of the unwelcome news.

The same day Major-General Frederick D. Middleton had an interview with Adolphe P. Caron, Minister of the Militia

---

Tacitus' Ann., Bk. II., 9 and 10.

and Defence, and left that night for Winnipeg, where he arrived on Friday, the 27th instant, ostensibly on the routine of his department. Upon the train between Ottawa and Winnipeg he heard of the battle of Duck Lake.

Major Crozier, of the mounted police, with about eighty of that force and forty volunteers under Captain Moore, together with the Scotch half-breed, Mackay, before mentioned, were on their way from Carleton to Duck Lake, the object of their journey being to secure the merchandise in Stobert, Eden & Co.'s store, together with a large amount of government supplies also lying at Duck Lake, destined for Chaffee, the Indian farm instructor near that place. These Major Crozier intended to convey to Prince Albert for safe keeping. But the insurgents had stolen a march upon them and seized everything the day previous. Major Crozier came upon the half-breeds on Beardy's Reserve, about two miles from Duck Lake. Here the first battle of the Saskatchewan war was fought. The number of the rebel force has been variously represented by their enemies as from 150 to 220. It is utterly impossible that there could have been even the minimum number of half-breeds upon the ground at the fight. The strength of their Indian auxiliaries is uncertain. The entire rebel force probably outnumbered the mounted police and volunteers by a score or more. There were not more than twenty engaged in the fight, the remainder being held in reserve. The insurgents were armed mostly with shotguns. The men on both sides were experts in guerilla and prairie warfare. The only substantial advantage, on the rebel side, was the fact that Dumont was a better general than Crozier. There are many published accounts of this battle. They are all by Englishmen, or Americans in the last stages of Anglomania. The poor half-breeds, like the ancient Cilicians, had no historians. If we believe some British writers, Riel and Dumont had more men in their little army than there were half-breeds in the Saint Laurent settlement, men, women and children included.   When Crozier came upon the insurgents they were standing behind a fringe of scrub poplar, near the edge of a coulee-ravine, with a stream running through it. At the word of command the government forces pointed their rifles at the insurgents.   Gabriel Dumont shouted: "Is it to be a fight?"   Crozier replied: "I must shoot if you do not lay down your arms."   Dumont picked up the gauntlet; and, without further parley, his men dropped into the ravine, and leveled their rifles along the top.   At this time Crozier, who was about three hundred yards away, held up his hand; and the police and volunteers extended their lines.   Crozier's men fired first.   The insurgents returned the shot, directing their fire to Crozier's left, where the Prince Albert volunteers were stationed, and eight of them fell.   This was undoubtedly intentional on the part of the insurgents, as they looked upon a policeman as only acting in line of his duty; but they regarded the volunteer as a traitor to the common cause.   After firing for half an hour, in a heavy fall of snow, it became evident to Crozier that the half-breeds were masters of the situation.   The discomfited Major retreated, with a loss of fourteen killed, and nine wounded.   The insurgents lost five killed.

At Fort Carleton Crozier met Colonel Irvine, with one hundred mounted police.   The old fort, whose surrender had been previously refused upon Riel's demand, was evacuated and burned.   At its destruction it wanted but two years to complete the first century of its existence.   The police retired down the river to Prince Albert.

The effect of this victory of the half-breeds was to arouse the Indians.   Battleford was besieged by the Sweet Grass and Poundmaker bands of Crees; and the settlers were forced to flee to the barracks, while the Indians looted their houses, acting more like a herd of swine than like human beings.

Three days after the fight at Duck Lake, Payne, farm instructor near Battleford, was murdered in the most fiendish manner by the Indians under his tutorage.

Thank God! the purpose of this volume does not require a detailed account of the horrible massacre at Frog Lake, as this was in no manner traced to Riel's door. Frog Lake is situated on the North side of the northern branch of the Saskatchewan, far up the stream, above Fort Pitt, a station of the mounted police, and near the foot of Moose Hills, so-called. The massacre was the bloody work of Big Bear's band of Crees, who have their reserve at Long Lake, the source of Beaver River, lying several days' journey north-west of Frog Lake. Big Bear, whom Mercer Adam styles the Pontiac of the North-West, exercised a tacit dominion over all the various bands of Indians in the vicinity of Long, Stoney, and Frog Lakes. On the third of April, Good Friday, the Indians, under Big Bear and Wandering Spirit, attacked the settlement at Frog Lake; interrupted the Holy Sacrifice of Mass; murdered several whites, including Thomas Quinn, Indian agent; two oblate fathers, Farfard and Marchard; John Delany, farm instructor, and John A. Gowanlock, millwright. They made prisoners of the wives of Delany and Gowanlock. For two long months these heroic women suffered the horrors of a captivity, whose history reads like the tale of Hannah Dustin. Through the chivalric conduct of four half-breeds, particularly of John Pritchard, these poor women were saved from being the victims of savage lust—an alternative worse than death. It was Wandering Spirit who fired the first shot at Frog Lake, the one which killed Indian Agent Quinn. That stalwart savage appears to have been the real leader of the movement. He afterwards pleaded guilty of murder, before Judge Rouleau; received his sentence, and justly suffered the law's extremest penalty for his terrible crime.

Thus have the salient features of this terrible affair been given. All allusion to it would have been avoided, but for the fact, that Riel was charged with being responsible for this masssacre. These accusers are about as just as were the northern fire-eaters who charged Jefferson Davis with being responsible for Little Crow's butcheries in Minnesota in 1862; or some other equally brilliant geniuses who blamed Roscoe Conkling for the act of Guiteau.   There is no doubt, but that Columbus was indirectly responsible for the killing of Montezuma.   If Columbus had not discovered America Montezuma would not have met his death in the peculiar manner that he did.   This is precisely the logic by which Riel's enemies would convict him of responsibility for the massacre at Frog Lake.   " The Indians never would have arisen, but for the half-breed revolt," they say; "they caught the contagion." Profundity of logic !   But for the American Revolution there would have never been a French Revolution. Hence it is obvious, that Thomas Jefferson was personally responsible for the judicial murder of Madame Roland.

It will be shown hereafter, that there was not sufficient legal proof, that Louis Riel instigated Poundmaker to go upon the war-path. Yet there is plenty of historical evidence of the fact.   The ethical propriety of a gentleman of Christian culture instigating a lot of irresponsible savages to deeds of blood is a matter upon which there ought to be but one opinion.   It is, surely, a course of conduct which could only be justified by the most intense provocation—something as terrible as that which provoked the negroes of Santo Domingo or the Sans-chulottes of 1789.

Riel had a bad example set, for him, by such elegant gentlemen as Doctor Schultz and General Burgoyne.   The story of the former has been related in this volume.   The latter was far more directly responsible for the murder of Jane McCrea than was Louis Riel for any outrage committed by Poundmaker's band.

Here, again, one weight and one measure are commended, for the Canadian, the Englishman and the half-breed alike.

It was out of the chronological order, to speak of the massacre at Frog Lake, at this particular time.   But, leaving the episode, let the campaign of Middleton, or a part of it be considered. No military history will be attempted here. Not even an epitome of the entire campaign will be given. At some future time the author will visit the North-West for the purpose of making a critical and strategical study of Middleton's campaign in that region, after which he will write an account of it. This campaign may be divided in three parts. First, the march from Qu'Appelle to Clark's Crossing; second, the campaign against the half-breeds, upon the Saskatchewan, including the battles of Fish Creek and Batoche; third, the subsequent Indian war, including the capture of Poundmaker, the pursuit of Big Bear, Loon Lake, and-so-forth. The first two are all that will be dealt with in this volume.

As already stated, General Middleton arrived at Winnipeg on the 27th of March, and on the evening of that day he started for Qu'Appelle with 260 men of the 90th Battalion. He arrived there the same day, and the 28th, 29th and 30th were devoted to those preliminaries indispensable to a long march. Students fitting for an American college usually read Homer's Iliad to the Catalogue of the Ships and stop there. I fear such would be the fate of this little book did the author stop here to give a detailed account of General Middleton's forces. His troops were made-up of citizen-soldiers, men who had left the shop, the desk and the farm. They were strangers to the barbaric art of war. Many of them had never pulled a trigger. The militia of Canada was under the control of Adolphe P. Caron, who was a member of the Cabinet and responsible to Parliament. They were under the immediate command of Frederick D. Middleton, an officer holding the rank of colonel in the regular army of Great Britain and ranking as major-general of militia, with a salary of $4,000 a year. Both the minister and the general were men of superior ability. The first was the son of the distinguished Canadian statesman of that name; and was worthy of his sire.

Frederick D. Middleton (a name which sounds well without a title) was the third son of Major-General Charles Middleton of the regular army.   He was a native of the land of Sarsfield and Wellington, having been born at Belfast, County Antrim, November 4, 1825.   The lad was educated at the Royal Military College, and entered the army December 30, 1842.   He served with the 50th regiment in the war against the Maoris, and spent the years 1846 and 1847, or the greater portion thereof, in New Zealand.   Here the young officer received his baptism of fire; and an education in guerilla warfare which was destined to distinguish him in his old age. He was mentioned in dispatches, and received a medal.   Afterwards, serving in the Santhal Rebellion, he was mentioned in dispatches, and received the thanks of the government. He took part in the suppression of the Sepoy Mutiny of 1857 and 1859.   Space forbids a minute account of his honourable record as a soldier.   He served at the historic siege of Lucknow, with which every school-boy is familiar.   In the year 1861, at the time of the Trent affair, Middleton came to Canada, as Major of the 29th, where he remained till the withdrawal of the troops from the country.   He has received many decorations and titles which Americans have never learned to value.   We believe, with Burns, that, "Rank is but the guinea's stamp," and-so-forth, and with Pitt, who said that Nelson would live in history as the greatest naval hero the world had ever seen, and none would ask whether he were a viscount or an earl.*   So, too, will Middleton live in history as the peer of any Indian fighter that ever trod the soil of the North American continent since the days of Cortez, with the possible exception of Andrew Jackson.   Had the writer placed Middleton above them all, he might have been put down as wanting in national pride.   General Middleton came to Canada as the successor to General Luard in the autumn of 1884.   He had scarcely become acquainted with his posi-

---

* Southey's Life of Nelson.

tion and its requirements, when he was called to lead his raw recruits to a contest which would test their metal, as well as the ability of their great commander.

The militia of the Dominion consisted of all citizens capable of bearing arms, and was divided into four classes: *First.* All unmarried men and childless widowers between the ages of 18 and 45; *Second.* Married men, and widowers having children, between the ages of 18 and 30; *Third.* Married men, and widowers having children, between the ages of 30 and 45; *Fourth.* All between 45 and 60. General Middleton's army was made-up of the first class, as the law required each class to be exhausted in its turn, before a levy could be made upon the next, except in case of a general levy, in which event every citizen able to bear arms could be called out.

The character of Middleton's army has already been described. He has been tersely and truly called "the brave commander of brave men." To this array of prowess and patriotism there was one melancholy exception. It was the hireling butcher, the black sheep from the American flock—bought with British gold by the Queen's factor, Adolphe P. Caron. Oh, shame! that the name of England's great philanthropist should be borne by the ghoul with the Gatling gun. His dishonoured name shall not pollute this page. English writers have delighted in styling John Paul Jones a pirate, who would have fought under the colours of the Dey of Algiers, as soon as those of his own Christian nation. But the worst caricature upon the commander of the Bon Homme Richard, would be the faintest delineation of that stipendiary assassin and military harlot— the Dugald Dalgatty of the North-West. Arnold's betrayal of his country has made his name a synonym for treason. His poetic type is Alp, the Adrian renegade, who forswore his country and his faith But these men had deep personal wrongs. Although we can not justify nor even excuse them. The tale of what each of them suffered has made the one a Byronic hero, and excites a pang of pity at the mention of the other's name. There is the same difference between the Thug with the Gatling gun, and Arnold or Alp, that there is between a street-walker and the victim of misplaced-confidence. The only form of man, in fact or in fiction, which will depict the gladiator of the Saskatchewan, is the Yahoo of Swift's creation. It was the irony of fate which gave to the second century of our national independence the humiliating spectacle of an American citizen playing the *role* of a Hessian.

The Gatling gun, named from its inventor, Doctor Richard J. Gatling, is an American invention which came a little too late to be of much service in the late war. A description would consume too much space, and be foreign to the purpose. Suffice to say, that its utility for frontier warfare is no longer a problem of pyrotechnics, but a fixed fact. A gun of this description was procured from the Gatling Company, of which the inventor was president. A carriage-maker from New Haven was found to go along and explain its working. This fellow is said to have been a soldier in the United States. If so, history has failed to record his exploits.

On the sixth of April, General Middleton set out with his army upon the celebrated march from Qu'Appelle to Batoche, by way of Touchwould Hills, the great Salt Plain, Humboldt and Clarke's Crossing, the last-named place being his objective point upon the Saskatchewan. The distance from Qu'Appelle to Clarke's Crossing is 177 miles. This march was accomplished in twelve days, being a trifle less than fifteen miles a day, including halts.

When we reflect, that Middleton's men were raw recruits; that the weather was inclement, it being the most disagreeable season of the year; that food for man and beast, as well as fuel for cooking, had to be transported; and when all the other draw-backs are remembered, Middleton's achievement appears wonderful. The nights were so cold, that the tent-pegs had to be chopped from the ground with axes. Yet the scarcity of fuel prevented the building of fires to warm the poor soldiers.

"Why," says some indolent lounger, "anybody can conduct a march." No military man would make that remark. Hannibal's march through Gaul, and his passage of the Alps have done more to immortalize his name than the combined glory of Cannae and Thrasymene.

General Middleton arrived at Clarke's Crossing on the 16th day of April, and the main body of his troops two days later.

It is worthy of remark, that, during the entire march, the troops were never harassed by the half-breeds or their Indian allies. Lord Melgund, General Middleton's chief of staff, writes:

"They [the half-breeds] never attacked a convoy, they never cut the wire behind us, and though Indians, and 'Breeds' are born mounted infantry, who can shoot as well from their horses as on foot, they never harassed us on the march."

After some remark about the earliness of the season, he adds:

"It would seem as if they intended only to defend their homes against invasion!" *

The reader would do well to remember this testimony from the military secretary of the notorious Marquis of Lansdowne. Melgund may be excused for misunderstanding Louis Riel, whom even Father Andre calumniated in the missionary journals of France. But it will be seen, that Lord Melgund's heart is not a stranger to generous and charitable thoughts.

Two days after General Middleton's arrival at Clarke's Crossing, he sent Colonel Otter, with the troops under his command, to Battleford. This was because of alarming reports, received from that quarter.

The general's description of the passage can not be improved. It is given intact:

* The Recent Rebellion in the North-West, *Nineteenth Century,* for August, 1885.

" I now determined to divide my small force and move down both sides of
the river, owing to the apparently correct information I had received that Riel's
force only numbered about 400 men all told, and the knowledge I possessed that
Lt.-Col. Irvine had over 200 under him at Prince Albert.   I commenced crossing over my left column, sending over French's scouts and half of Boulton's
mounted infantry by the two scows, which were now in working order.   The
second scow I procured from Saskatoon, the settlers of which place willingly
gave it up for the public service.   I would here beg to draw attention to the work
done by the troops to enable me to cross this column. The scow had to be made
water-tight ; the wire rope spliced, taken over and anchored to the other side ; a
platform and windlass erected on near side, to stretch the rope ; oars had to be
made with axes, wharves constructed, roads built down the steep banks to the
water edge, which was completely blocked by enormous blocks of solid ice im-
bedded in the thickest and stickiest of mud, the river running at the rate of four
miles an hour; and all this had to be done in very cold weather."[*]

The two columns then moved down the river, the division
on the left bank under command of Lord Melgund; the one
on the right was commanded by General Middleton himself.

On the 24th the column upon the right bank encountered
the half-breeds, under Gabriel Dumont, at a place called Fish
Creek.   The other division came to their assistance, when a
hard battle was fought.

A proper understanding of this engagement demands a preliminary explanation.

The south branch of the Saskatchewan has no valley strictly speaking. Although there are at rare intervals, low stretches
of bottom.   The course of the river would hardly be misnamed canon.   It flows through high prairie land.   The banks
of the stream and the adjacent country are cut by ravines,
through which rivulets feed the main stream from either side.

About eight miles above Batoche, on the right bank of the
river is a coulee, some forty feet in depth.   The bottom of the
ravine is one-fourth of a mile in width, and heavily timbered.

At this point the half-breeds, resolved to make a stand.   Dumont had planned to draw Middleton into an ambuscade.   It
was the snare with which Arminius had destroyed the Roman

[*] Report, Appendix No. 1, p. 3.

legions under Varius. Had it proved successful, the fight at
Fish Creek would have been a repetition of Braddock's defeat.
But a greater than Varius or Braddock was there.

The hardy old soldier had not fought the Maori for nothing.
He kept his scouts in advance of the main line. These turned
every copse, and explored every cranny.

On the night of the 23rd, the general halted near the farm
of a settler named McIntosh. On the morning of the 24th
the army began moving, about seven. The usual precautions
were observed. The mounted scouts were well in the advance; and spread out (to prevent the possibility of a successful ambuscade) in the front and flank. About two hundred
yards behind these followed Boulton's mounted infantry. The
advance guard of the 90th Battalion followed about two hundred yards in the rear of that; and the main column in about
two hundred and fifty yards behind the advance. Fish Creek
was six miles distant from the McIntosh farm; the Canadians
received a fire from some bluffs on the left. This was provoked by the approach of the scouts. General Middleton did
not commit the military blunder of Sturgis, which caused the
disgraceful fiasco at Guntown, during our late war. Instead
of double-quicking the main body up to support his skirmish-
ers, he caused the flankers and files in front to fall back upon
his phalanx (so to speak), thus preventing confusion. After
advancing from the ravine the half-breeds retired again; and
kept up a galling fire. The commanding general was shot
through his Astrachan cap. He shouted to his raw recruits to
hold their heads erect; and pointing to the hole in his hat, he
told them, that but for sitting upright his brains would have
been knocked out. About two in the afternoon all firing
ceased, except an occasional shot from the ravine. The half-
breeds had constructed rifle-pits in rows, along the side of the
ravine, from which they picked-off the soldiers. The Canadian army retired from the coulee and that night they rested
beside its brink which, as they believed, contained the enemy.

The next day disclosed the fact, that Dumont had retired from Fish Creek; and adopting Napoleon's tactics at Mantua had left a few men behind for a blind. The stratagem had proved a success.

The loss of General Middleton's army was ten killed and forty wounded. Of Dumont's army two dead Sioux and over fifty dead ponies were found in the ravine. It was said, that, after the fight, nearly every soldier in the army of the Dominion claimed to have killed his man. Dumont denies that the half-breeds lost a man; and says, that he had only forty-seven men engaged in the fight. The general places the insurgent force at two hundred and eighty. It is probable, that Dumont did not include, in his statement, the auxiliary force of Indian warriors. General Middleton's force numbered four hundred and seven; not one had ever been under fire before. The general has had many wiseacre critics of his course, in not charging upon the insurgents in the coulee, and for his general conduct of the battle. This is not the place to discuss these questions. Time, "the corrector when our judgments err," will vindicate the brave old commander. He said enough good men had fallen; and he was right.

The general placed the hole in his cap to the credit of Gabriel Dumont himself. But credited himself with a victory. There can be no doubt, but Middleton did everything at Fish Creek which a gallant soldier, an able commander could do. But, when it is claimed, that he won a victory, one feels almost like quoting Suwarrow's words, when he was saluted as a second Hannibal after his fight with Marshal Macdonald at Trebia: "Another such victory and we are ruined."

On the day following the battle the brave boys slain at Fish Creek were buried with the honours of war; and a cairn and a cross mark the spot.

> "Their requiem—the music of the river's surging tide;
> Their funeral wreaths—the wild flowers that grow on every side;
> Their monument—undying praise from each Canadian heart,
> That hears how, for their country's sake, they nobly bore their part."

On the 5th of May the steamer Northcote arrived from Swift Current (a station on the Canadian Pacific), having on board supplies, troops and the Gatling gun with the famous poltroon in command. Two days later the troops began to move upon Batoche, where the closing scene in this terrible drama was to be enacted. The general had brought his left column across the river to join his right.

The entire country between Gabriel's Crossing and Batoche was cut up into wooded ravines; some of them fifty feet in depth.

On the next day after leaving Fish Creek, the wily commander abandoned the dangerous trail along the river, and marching to the eastward, and then to the north-west, struck the trail from Humboldt to Batoche, about nine miles from the latter place, and camped for the night. As soon as the camp was selected, remembering the adage, " A good general provides for a retreat," Middleton pushed on with some of Boulton's mounted infantry to within four miles of Batoche, where he selected a site for a camp, in case it became necessary to fall back from Batoche.

In the deep and wooded ravines which surrounded this place, Nature had provided a formidable rampart. The half-breeds had added something to her fastnesses. The rifle-pit, an invention of civilized man, had been utilized by these guerilla warriors. These had been dug to the depth of ten feet; were located in the most strategic points, and in firm, sandy soil. They were always placed at the edge of woods, with the ground usually sloping to the rear, and extending upward or horizontally to the front. They were constructed with loop-holes made of logs and a ramp to descend by, with branches stuck into turned-up earth to conceal the pit. These rifle-pits form one of the most important strategical features of this singular campaign.

Never, since the little army of Leonidas made their stand at Thermopylæ against the myriads of Xerxes, has the world seen a more desperate and heroic defence than was made by the half-breeds at Batoche.

It is not claimed that in the war upon the Saskatchewan the advantages were all on one side. Far from it! The half-breeds had the advantage of being upon the defensive, of being skilled in prairie warfare, and of being under the leadership of a chief whose ability as a partisan commander has hardly been surpassed in the history of the world. There were other advantages, already mentioned, in the nature of the country and the rifle-pits.

The Canadians had the advantage of superior numbers; of arms, ammunition and artillery; of a commander with a varied experience in all kinds of warfare; of the moral force of an established government at their backs, and last, but not least, the Gatling gun.

Here one can not forget the irreverent remark of Napoleon, that God is always on the side of the heaviest artillery.

Any one familiar with the history of Schamyl's war against the Tsar, or the campaign of the old Spanish chief Sartorius, while contending with the armies of Rome, will understand that superior numbers are not always an insurmountable advantage.

On the morning of the 9th of May, 1885, the army under General Middleton left their camp standing and moved upon Batoche. They pushed on without opposition to the point where the Humboldt trail struck the river before turning down to Batoche, about one-half mile from the Catholic church. Between this place and the church there were three houses, near which some men were standing. A discharge from the Gatling gun dispersed them, and the Canadians moved slowly toward the church. From a house upon the further side of the church a white flag was being displayed. The general rode up to this, and found three or four priests, some sisters of charity, and half-breed women and their children.

The church of Saint Anthony of Padua looks down upon the valley, or, rather, plain of Batoche, which is an elliptical basin, surrounded by a ridge broken by wooded ravines. In the bluffs around this basin the half-breeds had entrenched themselves in the rifle-pits, before described.

The artillery was placed to command the position of the half-breeds, and a discharge of shell and shot was opened upon the little hamlet of Batoche. The buildings were light and the consequent injury was not great. A sudden and unexpected fire was received from the insurgent sharp-shooters who were concealed. The discharge was accompanied by a whoop, but the shot was too high. Yet the surprise almost caused a stampede among the Canadians. A rush from the desperate insurgents had nearly captured the Canadian battery, when Captain Peters came up with the Gatling gun; and the New Haven carriage-maker seized the crank, and scattered the terrible missiles of destruction upon the little band of patriots with the brutal remark: " I'll show you how to take guns." This murderous volley was followed by a harvest of death, shocking to any one but the biped who sowed the seed.

" In vain, alas! in vain! Ye gallant few!"

The battery guns were removed beyond the reach of the discomfited insurgents.

A detailed account of this and the three subsequent days' fighting will be reserved for another work, before mentioned. Suffice it to say, that the sun went down on the evening of the 9th of May, 1885, and witnessed no substantial advantage to either of the contending armies at Batoche. The troops bivouacked upon the field; and slept with their guns in their hands.

The following day was Sunday, which passed without incident, save the bombardment of a grave-yard by the Winnipeg battery.

The next day was " as the last was, as the next [apparent-

7

ly] would be." The half-breeds remained steadfastly in their rifle-pits. At evening General Middleton might have addressed his troops, in the words of Zachary Taylor at Palo Alto: "My hardy cocks, the bayonet is the thing."

The day following, while planning a general and decided attack, Middleton distinguished a white flag at a point in the enemy's lines. The bearer was Astley, one of Riel's prisoners, who was also the bearer of the following note:

"BATOCHE.

"If you massacre our families, we are going to massacre the Indian agent and other prisoners.

"LOUIS 'DAVID' RIEL,
"Exovede."

"Per J. W. Astley, bearer, *May 12th, 1885.*

This was taken as a confession of weakness; and the general replied as follows:

"*May 12th, 1885.*

"MR. RIEL—I am anxious to avoid killing women and children and have done my best to avoid doing so. Put your women and children in one place and let us know where it is, and no shot shall be fired on them. I trust to your honor not to put men with them.

"FRED. MIDDLETON,
"*Com. N. W. Field Forces.*"

The forenoon was passed in firing between sharp-shooters on either side. The men took their dinner in the trenches. In the afternoon a general advance was made; and the half-breeds were driven from their rifle-pits to the cemetery. A portion of the Canadian troops entered a ravine which encircled the cemetery, and shot the half-breeds in the rifle-pits, bayoneted the survivors in their vain attempt at flight. At this time the general received a call from Astley, who was the bearer of another note. It read:

"BATOCHE, *12th May, 1885.*

"*Major-General Middleton:*

"GENERAL—Your prompt answer to my note shows that I was right in mentioning to you the cause of humanity. We will gather our families in one place, and as soon as it is done we will let you know.

"I have the honor to be, General,

"Your humble servant,

"LOUIS 'DAVID' RIEL.."

Upon the envelope was the following, in Riel's hand-writing, but without signature:

> "I do not like war, and if you do not, retreat and refuse an interview, the question remaining the same, the prisoners."

The general replied, that his troops would cease firing when the enemy did, and not before. After this Riel's little band of patriots fought with the courage born of despair. But it was all in vain, the bayonet and the Gatling did the work. The village was carried, Riel's council house was captured; and his prisoners were released. The chief and his lieutenant escaped. The latter flew to the United States.

Three days, afterward, Riel surrendered himself to two scouts, Hourie and Armstrong. This surrender was made on the strength of a letter received from General Middleton, promising, in effect, as the general testified, protection from immediate violence, and a trial by law. Honourable Edward Blake comments as follows:

> "Now the Honourable Minister of Militia (Adolphe P. Caron) referred to what he called the evidence with regard to the letter of General Middleton to Riel; yet he did not satisfy me that Riel did not surrender on that letter. The statement of Colonel Boulton was directly to the contrary, and if we remember the whole circumstances of the case—the time General Middleton wrote the letter, and the condition of things stated by the First Minister in one of the discussions last session as to papers—I do not think that is a fair inference from the evidence. But the Honourable Minister said he would prove the purpose for which the letter was given, and he proved it by reading a letter from the Major-General, who, he said, had been told by some one that Riel was afraid of being killed in the camp. That was not very good evidence against Riel, as the honourable gentleman knows. The intent with which General Middleton sent the letter is of no consequence. The question is, what does the letter fairly import. The authority of General Middleton is not of any consequence, if that were disputed, though I do not suppose it is. Now, the question, to my mind, on this subject is just this: Is it for the honour and credit of the volunteers of Canada that it should be declared that that paper was sent in order to warrant the prisoner, if he surrendered himself, against lynch law? Is it to the credit and honour of the volunteers to say that it was necessary for a Major-General in the British army, to give assurance to Riel and his council that they would not be lynched if they surrendered themselves. I should be sorry to come to any

such conclusion; and then, the question remains: Was it not reasonable to believe that the result of this statement was, You shall not, in fact, be exposed to the very worst that you can possibly be exposed to if you are caught—that is, death. I think the liberal interpretation of that letter, in the sense and spirit in which such letters and assurances have been interpreted in all events of this description, would have led to that conclusion."*

The text of this letter has never come to the knowledge of the writer, and, always having been an admirer of the old general, he would probably be a prejudiced judge. Throughout the late difficulty in the North-West the author looked at the general with the eyes of love and enthusiastic admiration, and regarded him as the moral Agamemnon who towered above the others.

Louis Riel was taken down the Saskatchewan on the Northcote and was placed in custody of an escort under command of Captain Young of the Winnipeg Field Battery, and sent to Regina, by way of Humboldt, there to await the further pleasure of the Dominion government. The Reverend Pitblado of Winnipeg accompanied the escort. This gentleman, although he did not regard Riel as a great soldier, repelled the charge of cowardice made against him.

Riel was confined at the Mounted Police Barracks, about two miles from the city. After being kept there for about two months, he was brought for trial before Honourable Hugh Richardson,† a stipendiary magistrate.

This gentleman has been the victim of ridicule and the target of abuse from every champion of Riel and his cause. An editorial found in the *Springfield Republican,*‡ entitled, "*Canada's Condemned Traitor,*" describes him as: "A bushy-whiskered, big-necked frontier justice." This is all wrong.

* See the *Hansard.*

† It is true there was a justice of the peace, named Henry Le Jeune sitting with Mr. Justice Richardson, but the former reminds the writer of one of the side judges they used to have in the State of Vermont—a judicial nonentity.

‡ See weekly issue for August 7, 1885.

Lieutenant-Colonel Hugh Richardson was, at the time of the trial, in his sixtieth year. He was called to the bar when he was twenty-one years old; and was engaged in active practice for twenty-nine years; during five he held the position of County Attorney. For nine years he had been Stipendiary Magistrate, a position whose importance has, already, been described. He is a native of England; and a gentleman of learning, firmness and integrity. If occasion is found to criticise the conduct of Riel's trial, the fault lies deeper than the character or the ability of the magistrate himself. It must be sought in the accursed judicial system itself. Now the writer will not retract a syllable of the first part of his work. But he will say, some things by way of supplement.

Professor Bryce, in his able work before cited, under the title, " Pure Justiciary," expresses himself as follows:

"One of the great advantages of the province over the neighbouring states is in the administration of justice. In the United States the judges are elected by the people directly. Accordingly, if the judge be elected by the Republicans, he is expected to deal out hard measure to the Democrats, and *vice versa*. The result of this is simply frightful. Such a thing as gaining fair play from a judge of adverse political opinions is not counted on in many parts of the United States. This gives rise to a vast amount of trickery and collusion in business."

. . . . . . "The Canadian of the present day looks with great pleasure on the high character and impartiality of the bench of Canada. It is the English law which prevails. The dignity of the court is maintained by the use of a suitable costume, and the authority of the bench is paramount. The appearance of American courts, where the lawyers appear in grey clothing if they choose, and assume the most ' free and easy ' manners, is absolutely distressing. It is related to have occurred in Kansas that a court crier, in adjourning the court, did so in the following words, 'O yes! O yes! O yes! This whole outfit will adjourn till to-morrow morning.' " *

There is a plain, though expressive, Saxon word of three letters; but it is more forcible than elegant. The writer dislikes to use it, while the ugly monster almost forces itself upon his lips. Had he the style of a Junius he might picture, without naming, a man whose heart could conceive, whose

* Manitoba: Its Infancy, Growth and Present Condition, page 357.

brain could engender, and whose hand could pen such fact-
less things.   The Manitoba professor must have taken the fiction of the Kansas court-crier (an officer, by the by, unknown in the States) from some comic almanac.

The author will enter upon no defence of the elective judiciary system.   For he does not, and never did believe in it.
It has been fittingly described as "democracy run mad."
But, with all its faults, the elective system is far better than
the judiciary that exists (like the judiciary which tried Riel)
during the pleasure of the government whose creature it is.
This elective system may have a tendency to demagogism,
and, in some instances does create judicial charlatans, like
Absalom, who would be judge in Israel.

But even Absalom is preferable to Jeffreys.

It is not meant to abuse Colonel Richardson; but it must be
insisted that he is human.   He held an office whose tenure was
dependent upon the good pleasure of the administration at
Ottawa.   He was the secretary, or clerk, and the legal adviser
of the North-West Council.   He was receiving a salary from
the Dominion of $3,000, augmented by perquisites to nearly
$2,000 more.   If he was able to sit in the case, and preside
without bias, he was certainly a very superior man, one whose
like the world has hardly seen since the days of Aristides.   Yet
it must be admitted that he succeeded better than most men
would have done.

Riel was brought to trial upon an information verified and
filed by Alexander David Stewart, Chief of Police of Hamilton, Ontario.   The information contained six counts.   The
following counsel appeared for the Crown: Messrs. Robinson, Osler, Scott, Casgrain and Burbidge, Deputy Minister
of Justice.

The prisoner was defended by Francis X. Lemieux, Charles
Fitzpatrick and Messrs. Johnston and Greenshields.

From the outset it was evident that the Government was
determined to have the prisoner's blood.   A large number of

half-breeds had been captured. But all of these, save Riel, had been charged simply with treason-felony, a crime punishable only with perpetual imprisonment, while Riel had been charged with high treason, the punishment of which was death. The reason for this was so plain that he who runs may read. Behind the scenes stood the Nemesis of Thomas Scott. There were in Ontario two thousand Orange lodges clamouring for the blood of Riel. Only the life of a wild enthusiast descended from a "very mixed stock of Indians, half-breeds and Irish whites," lay between Sir John A. Macdonald and the united support of the Orangemen of Ontario. The Dominion Government was the prosecutor in a higher sense than the mere title of the cause would imply. Riel's trial was emphatically a state trial. It reminds one of the days of the Earl of Essex or of Lady Alice Lisle. This tyrant's plea of state necessity was eloquently and nobly described by Franklin Pierce, afterwards President of the United States, in a speech before the Federal Senate:

" Sir, this demand of the nation,—this plea of state of necessity,—let me tell gentlemen, is as old as the history of wrong and oppression. It has been the standing plea, the never-failing resort of despotism.

" The great Julius found it a convenient plea when he resorted the *dignity* of the Roman Senate, but destroyed its *independence*. It gave countenance to, and justified, all the atrocities of the Inquisition in Spain. It forced out the stifled groans that issued from the Black Hole of Calcutta. It was written in tears upon the Bridge of Sighs in Venice, and pointed to those dark recesses upon whose gloomy thresholds there was never seen a returning footprint.

" It was the plea of the austere and ambitious Strafford, in the days of Charles I. It filled the Bastile of France, and lent its sanction to the terrible atrocities perpetrated there. It was this plea that snatched the mild, eloquent and patriotic Camille Desmoulins from his young and beautiful wife and hurried him to the guillotine, with thousands of others, equally unoffending and innocent. It was upon this plea that the greatest of generals, if not men,—you cannot mistake me,—I mean him, the presence of whose very ashes, within the last few months, sufficed to stir the hearts of a continent,—it was upon this plea that he abjured the noble wife who had thrown light and gladness around his humbler days, and, by her own lofty energies and high intellect, had encouraged his aspirations. It was upon this plea that he committed that worst and most fatal act of his eventful life. Upon this, too, he drew around his person the imperial purple. It has in all times, and in every age, been the foe of liberty, and the indispensable stay of usurpation.

"Where were the chains of despotism ever thrown around the freedom of speech and of the press but on this plea of STATE OF NECESSITY? Let the spirit of Charles X. and of his ministers answer.

"It is cold, selfish, heartless, and has always been regardless of age, sex, condition, services, or any of the incidents of life that appeal to patriotism or humanity. Wherever its authority has been acknowledged, it has assailed men who stood by their country when she needed strong arms and bold hearts, and has assailed them when, maimed and disabled in her service, they could no longer brandish a weapon in her defence. It has afflicted the feeble and dependent wife for the imaginary faults of the husband. It has stricken down Innocence in its beauty, Youth in its freshness, Manhood in its vigor, and Age in its feebleness and decrepitude."*

The trial began on the 20th of July. The prisoner's counsel made an abortive attempt to obtain a continuance for the purpose of procuring testimony. One part of the testimony described in the application was a certificate of Riel's naturalization. An adjournment of one week was finally agreed upon. The question of citizenship was afterwards totally ignored by counsel and court.

Thomas D. Rambaut, of the New York bar, has written a pamphlet of 167 pages. The object of the book is the antithesis of this. This profound writer takes the trouble to inform his readers that, preliminary to the trial of Riel, "No coroner's inquest had been held nor indictment found by the grand jury." What, in the name of all that is mysterious, would they hold a coroner's inquest upon in a case of high treason! The body politic? Such questions are fathomless for ordinary mortals, and must be reserved for members of the New York bar.

On the 28th day of July the trial began in earnest. Counsellor Osler opened on behalf of the Crown. The prosecution called fourteen witnesses, who testified as to the affair at Duck Lake and the battles of Fish Creek and Batoche.

* Hawthorne's Life of Pierce, pp. 42–44.

Doctor Willoughby, of Saskatoon, and Thomas Mackay, of Prince Albert, were the chief witnesses to prove the animus of Riel from declarations made by him. General Frederick D. Middleton and John W. Astley were the chief witnesses to prove Riel's leadership and direction of the rebellion. There was much documentary evidence, among other things a letter in Riel's handwriting found in Poundmaker's camp. No proper foundation was laid for the introduction of this document, its receipt by Poundmaker not having been shown. When Robinson came to sum-up the case for the Crown he made use of this language:

" My learned friend, Mr. Fitzpatrick, must have forgotten what is due to a prisoner when he charged those who were acting for the Crown with some warmth for not having called Poundmaker to prove the receipt of that document. He was good enough at the same time to say that those who were conducting the case for the Crown were persons who understood fair play. It was because we did understand fair play, because it would have been improper to have called Poundmaker to swear to that, that we did not call him. If we had attempted to put Poundmaker in the box to prove the receipt of this document we should have been asking Poundmaker to declare on his oath his own complicity in this rebellion, and Poundmaker would have said to us: ' I decline to answer your questions,' and any judge would have said to those who acted for the Crown: ' Gentlemen, you had no business to put a man in that position.' Now that is our answer on the part of the Crown to the charge that we didn't call the prisoners to prove their own guilt out of their own mouth."

That is to say, when you can not lay the proper foundation for the introduction of a document, you are entitled to put it in any way.

The Crown utterly failed to show that either Duck Lake, Fish Creek or Batoche were within the Realm of Her Majesty. This was, probably, on the theory that Riel was a citizen of Great Britain, and, consequently, the proof of a venue was not necessary. Several Crown witnesses testified to Riel's abuse of prisoners. This was in contradiction of Lord Melgund, who wrote, that the half-breeds treated their prisoners well.*

---

* Article in the *Nineteenth Century*, August, 1885.

When the Crown witness Nolin was being cross-examined the defendant interfered in the management of the case by his lawyers, objecting to the plea of insanity. The court held, that once he had counsel he could not interfere.

Counsellor Greenshields opened on behalf of the prisoner. His speech is said to have been an eloquent and exhaustive history of the half-breed difficulties. The writer has never been able to procure a copy of it. For some reason the government at Ottawa have excluded it from their published documents. This reason is plain and clear. The defence sought to show the state of affairs in the Saskatchewan valley, the grievances of the half-breeds, and-so-forth. This testimony was excluded. The defence was compelled to fall back upon the plea of insanity. Riel's lawyers fought for him at Regina as bravely as did his half-breeds at Batoche. They called six witnesses to prove the prisoner's insanity.

One of these was Doctor Roy, who had treated Riel at Beauport asylum. There was another expert called by the prisoner's counsel, Doctor Clarke. The defence rested.

Then the Crown called seven witnesses to rebut the plea of insanity. Rambaut insists that the preponderance of testimony on this point was with the Crown. The rule, that the greater number of witnesses constitute the preponderance, must be something peculiar to New York practice.

Counsellor Fitzpatrick summed-up on behalf of the defendant, probably in as able a manner as the testimony would allow.

The prisoner was permitted to address the jury in his own behalf. The address is thus described by the *Springfield Republican*, in the editorial, "*Canada's Condemned Traitor*," before mentioned.

"If there was any favorable impression made at all upon the jury, it was the result of Riel's own bearing and words. When the evidence was all in he rose and made a remarkable plea of over two hours. It was a unique thing in oratory, his exordium consisting of an impressive prayer to Heaven to bless everybody in the case, and his peroration was short, logical and clever, he taking a paper from his pocket after his long speech and reading deliberately. When he sat down two of the jury were in tears, and of course all the women were. He first paid his eloquent respects to his legal advisers for pronouncing him insane, and then turning the case about and reviewing the refusal of the Dominion government to protect the half-breeds, he charged on the ministers themselves,—'insanity,' he added, 'complicated with paralysis.' He said that he had two mothers—the one who nursed him and the Northwest,—neither of whom would kill him. If there was any power in this man facing his jury, it was all contained in the patriotic sentiment of which he is the picturesque embodiment and which prompted him to admit his treason in order to protect 'my people in Saskatchewan.' By the rules of discretion that govern men on solemn trial for treason Louis Riel is wanting, just as common discretion was wanting in the great Socratic trial. He affronted the court, the Dominion, the Catholics, the very men that were detailed to defend him, and in fact everybody but his poor Metis nation. It was all madness, but the method of it will confirm his fame in the Northwest. For stern, audacious assumption of dignity, what can match his prayer to Heaven in behalf of all engaged in the trial,—'Turn curiosity into calm interest. Amen!'"*

Counsellor Robinson closed on behalf of the Crown. His address is the ablest argument against a plea of insanity it has ever been the author's good fortune to read. There is one passage in his speech noteworthy because of its sophistry:

"The Crown's witness, Charles Nolin, had testified: 'He [Riel] spoke of money, I think he said he wanted $10,000 or $15,000. The first time he spoke about it he did not know of any particular plan to get it, at the same time he told me that he wanted to claim an indemnity from the Canadian government. He said that the Canadian government owed him about $100,000, and then the question arose whom the persons were whom he would have to talk to the government about the indemnity. Some time after that the prisoner told me that he had an interview with Father Andre and that he had made peace with the church, that since his arrival in the country he had tried to separate the people from the clergy, that until that time he was at open war almost with the clergy. He said that he went to the church with Father Andre and in the presence of another priest and the Blessed Sacrament he had made peace, and said that he would never again do anything against the clergy. Father Andre told him he would use his influence with the government to obtain for him $35,000. He said that he would be content with $35,000 then and that he would settle with the government himself for the balance of $100,000. That agreement took place at Prince Albert. The agreement took place at Saint Laurent and then Father Andre went back to his mission at Prince Albert.' "†

Springfield Weekly Republican, August 7, 1885. †Queen *v.* Riel, p. 93.

Father Andre had testified:

" He [Riel] said, ' If I am satisfied, the half-breeds will be.' I must explain this. This objection was made to him that even if the government granted him $35,000 the half-breed question would remain the same, and he said in answer to that, ' If I am satisfied, the half-breeds will be.' "*

Mr. Robinson commented as follows:

" Now, in this case there is one absolutely conclusive fact proved, about which there can be no dispute, which is a complete answer to the defence of insanity. There is no question and no dispute of one thing, that the very essence of an insane impulse is that it is impervious to reason. The impulse of the insane man is such that you do not reason him into it and therefore you cannot reason him out of it. The moment you find the impulse which possesses a man yielding to reason, force or any motive, that moment that ceases to be an insane delusion." . . . . " Now, what are the facts here? We are told that this man's controlling mania was a sense of his own importance and power; that he was so possessed with overweening vanity and insane ambition, that the one thing that he was unable to resist, which in his own mind justified all crimes and was an atonement for all guilt, was his own sense of greatness and position and his power. Well, gentlemen, is it not a fact that he expressly said that if he could get a certain sum of money he would give up this power and this ambition and go away."†

The best answer to this is a passage from the speech of Honourable Edward Blake, delivered in the House of Commons, March 19th, 1886:

" In this connection I desire to say a word, and a word only, with reference to a charge highly calculated, if true, to increase the guilt, so far as he was morally responsible, of Riel. I refer to the charge of venality. I have already read that portion of the evidence of Nolin which shows the purpose to which this man stated he would apply the money which he was about to get from the Government—that he would apply it in starting a newspaper and in raising other nationalities in the States, and to effecting the prosecution of his designs. I say that however plainly that may appear to be a violent, a wicked, or a mad sentiment, it is utterly inconsistent with the charge of venality; it shows that this was the mode which, in his disordered mind, he thought would be most efficacious in order to accomplish the design for his people and for himself, as part of his purpose, which he entertained. But the very circumstance that he made that statement to Nolin, to my mind proves that it is impossible that he could have made the proposal for a venal purpose. I know perfectly the prejudices which exist. I know how many men would like to ease their consciences by

---

* Queen *v.* Riel, p. 113.   † Epitome of Parliamentary Documents, etc., p. 202.

saying: Oh, this was a base, and venal man. But it would be an act of humiliating cowardice on the part of one who has formed another conclusion on this subject, to bend to such prejudices, and to allow a name which must ever be deeply clouded and stained, to receive another cloud or stain, which he, at any rate, in my judgment, does not deserve. But I will add this, that I had expected to hear ere now from an honourable gentleman who was very intimately associated with Louis Riel, who worked together with Louis Riel in the North-West, his appreciation of that portion of the case. I have been told a story—I was told it by one who knew—on this subject. When the first intelligence came that he had asked the government for money, that he was going to sell the cause, 'Well,' I said 'this is a most extraordinary thing; it entirely alters the whole complexion of the case.' 'Oh, do not believe it,' said this gentleman who knew. 'Well,' I said, 'I have reason to believe that he has asked for the money.' 'Yes that is quite possible, he is quite convinced he has a claim, but depend upon it, I know that it is impossible that he can have asked for money to deceive or betray his people, or that he would betray their cause. I know all the events, which occurred when he was in the provincial government. I know that at the time when he was in power there in 1869-70, when he had the resources of the Hudson Bay Company at his command, his own family was in a state of destitution, living down at their place, and he would not allow any portion of what he called public property to be sent to them at all, even to keep them in life, and that same provisional council was obliged to secretly send down a bag of flour or something of that kind to his mother, who had the charge of the family, in order to keep them alive.'"

"An Honourable Member—Too thin."

"Mr. Blake—Somebody says, that it is too thin. I refer the honourable gentlemen to the honourable member for Provencher (Mr. Royal) on that subject."*

Judge Richardson, in his charge to the jury, used the following language:

"To assist you in your deliberations, let me draw your attention to some points suggested to my mind by the evidence. You recollect the statements as to the prisoner's appropriating property, and making prisoners of others simply because they, to his idea, opposed him in his movements. It has been suggested by the Crown, in reference to the $35,000, that it tends to show that this was all a scheme of the prisoner's to put money in his own pocket. Be that as it may, one of the witnesses, Nolin speaks distinctly as to the $35,000, and on that branch of his evidence we have his corroborated by the priest Father Andre

---

* This speech of the Liberal Leader is a masterpiece of its kind, an eloquent, exhaustive and logical exposition of the Riel question. At its close there is no aspect of this awkward affair which is untouched ; and little remains to be said upon the subject.

and further by Jackson. Then you have heard the evidence given by Captain Young as to the conversations he had with the prisoner. Witness after witness gave evidence as to what occurred in March, at the time of the commencement of this rebellion. Some of them speak of the prisoner being very irritable when the subject of religion was brought up. It appears, however, that his irritability had passed away when he was coming down with Captain Young, as we do not hear anything of it then. Does this show reasoning power?

"Then at what date can you fix this insanity as having commenced? The theory of the defence fixes the insanity as having commenced only in March, but threats of what he intended to do began in December. Admitting that the insanity only commenced about the time of the breaking out of the rebellion, what does seem strange to me is that these people who were about him, if they had an insane man in their midst, that some of them had not the charity to go before a magistrate and lay an information setting forth that there was an insane man amongst them, and that a breach of the peace was liable to occur at any moment, and that he should be taken care of. I only suggest that to you, not that you are to take it as law, I merely suggest it to you as turning upon the evidence." *

Such language as that addressed to the jury from the bench, would be enough to reverse a conviction in any state of the American Union. It is not the fault of the judge so much as of the infernal English custom of the judge summing-up the evidence; that is, virtually telling the jury how to find.

After receiving the instructions of the court, the jury retired to deliberate, and while they were out the prisoner engaged in prayer in the box. He sat upon each juryman's seat, and prayed fervently; then he sprinkled the seats with holy water. In a half-hour the jury returned a verdict of guilty, with a recommendation to mercy.

Riel was asked, as is usual, if he had anything to say why the sentence of the law should not be pronounced upon him. He spoke for two hours with much eloquence, reviewing his life, and the grievences of his race. But, as in such cases generally, he offered no legal objection to the sentence. The court then addressed the prisoner:

"Louis Riel, after a long consideration of your case, in which you have been defended with as great ability as I think any counsel could have defended you

* Epitome of Parliamentary Documents, pp. 211 and 212.

with, you have been found by a jury who have shown, I might almost say, un-
exampled patience, guilty of a crime, the most pernicious and greatest that man
can commit; you have been found guilty of high treason, you have been proved
to have let loose the flood-gates of rapine and bloodshed, you have, with such
assistance as you had in the Saskatchewan country, managed to arouse the Indians and have brought ruin and misery to many families whom if you had
simply left alone, were in comfort and many of them were on the road to afflu-
ence. For what you did, the remarks you have made form no excuse whatever;
for what you have done the law requires you to answer.

" It is true that the jury in merciful consideration, have asked Her Majesty
to give your case such merciful consideration as she can bestow upon it. I had
almost forgotten that those who are defending you have placed in my hands a
notice that the objection which they raised at the opening of the court must not
be forgotten from the records, in order that, if they see fit, they may raise the
question in the proper place. That has been done; but in spite of that I can
not hold out any hope to you that you will succeed in getting entirely free, or
that Her Majesty will, after what you have been the cause of doing, open her
hand of clemency to you. For me, I have only one more duty to perform; that
is, to tell you what the sentence of the law is upon you. I have, as I must, given
time to enable your case to be heard. All I can suggest or advise you is to prepare to meet your end; that is all the advice or suggestion I can offer. It is my
painful duty to pass the sentence of the court upon you, and that is that you be
taken now from here to the police guard room at Regina, which is the jail and
place from whence you came, and that you be kept there till the 18th of September next, and on the 18th of September next you be taken to the place appointed for your execution and there be hanged by the neck till you are dead.
And may God have mercy on your soul!"*

A friend of Riel writes the author, on this part of the
trial:

" The judge's sentence was accompanied by remarks so brutal that they have
been suppressed from the official record. See the reports of the contemporary
press."

After the condemnation of Riel an appeal was taken to the
court of Queen's Bench of Manitoba.

The errors assigned were in substance:

I. That the law giving a stipendiary magistrate, with a justice of the peace, and a jury of six power to try a prisoner
was contrary to *Magna Charta.*

II. That the law required the information to be taken be-

* Queen *v.* Riel, page 166.

fore a stipendiary magistrate and a justice of the peace, instead of the stipendiary alone.

III. That the law required the magistrate to take the testimony in writing; and a short-hand reporter's notes were not a compliance with the statute.

IV. That the evidence was insufficient.

V. That the powers of the Dominion Parliament were delegated, not plenary; and their act was *ultra vires.*

John S. Ewart, Francis X. Lemieux and Charles Fitzpatrick appeared for Riel. His counsel demanded, that he be brought to Winnipeg, to be present in court, while the appeal was heard, but this request was denied.

Messrs. Robinson, Osler and Aikens, Queen's Counsellors, appeared for the Crown. The conviction was sustained. This opinion was delivered upon the 9th of September, just nine days before the fatal day. The judges, Wallbridge, Taylor and Killam, delivered separate opinions.

As this was a capital offense, the prisoner had the right to petition the Privy Counsel for an appeal. This was done, and a respite was obtained for the purpose of presenting the petition. The proceedings upon such appeal were conducted by Messrs. Lemieux and Fitzpatrick of counsel for Riel. The petition was dated September 14. On the 24th of October an official telegram announced that the appeal had been denied.

The only hope of the doomed man seemed now to rest upon executive clemency on the part of the Dominion Government, or interference on the part of the United States.

A reprieve was given till November. This was lengthened until the 16th of that month, on the request of high ecclesiastical authority, the suspense in which the prisoner had been kept having unfitted him for making the proper preparation for the great change before him.

The government at Ottawa had been engaged in a prolonged conspiracy, of six months duration, having for its ob-

ject the death of this man. They sought, however, to give
to their acts the colour of justice. At the request of Riel's
friends, a commission was appointed to examine into the question of his sanity. This commission was one not calculated
to favour the prisoner. It is true that General Middleton, at
Riel's trial, testified to his sanity. But it must be remembered
that, although an excellent judge in military matters, the old
general had never distinguished himself as a medical expert.
His judgment in cases of deceptive insanity, like megalomania,
is of little value. A man may be perfectly sane on every subject, save one, and insane upon that one. This is monomania,
a species of insanity recognized in the days of Shakspere and
Cervantes. Every one knows the story related in the second
part of Don Quixote of the licentiate of Ossuna, confined by
his friends in the mad-house at Seville. He was believed to
have been restored to reason, but, as he was leaving the asylum, in a discourse with a fellow patient, he betrayed the condition of the unrestored madman. The only testimony of
any even apparent value to the sanity of Riel was that of
Doctor Jukes. This gentleman, in effect, stated that Riel was
insane on " purely religious questions having relation to what
may be called divine mysteries."

Such testimony shows the value of cross-examination. To
a person reading between the lines, it is plain that Jukes regarded Riel as a monomaniac, exactly what was contended
for on his behalf.

The ablest argument in favour of the theory of insanity,
and against the conduct of the government, is the speech of
Honourable Edward Blake, from which the author has already quoted. The argument is learned and exhaustive.

There can be no doubt that Riel, though ostensibly about
to be hanged for high treason, was really to suffer for the
" murder " of Scott. The Honourable John S. D. Thompson,
Minister of Justice, said upon this subject:

" The policy of considering what the past history of the convict has been is

S

one which is recognized, not only in the practice of every tribunal administering criminal justice, but is recognized by Parliament as well."*

The Macdonald government tried to sneak behind the miserable subterfuge that Riel's amnesty was conditional upon his remaining in banishment five years; that this had been violated, because, during his confinement at the Beauport asylum, he was not in banishment. The idea of a lunatic breaking a compact is too absurd to deserve a serious answer.

The Peace Society of London had solicited Her Majesty's interference in vain.

The last hope was action by the government at Washington. Bayard, President Cleveland's Secretary of State, had stated that the government would not intervene unless asked to do so.

The government refused to investigate the question of Riel's citizenship.

Rambaut, in a foot note, makes this statement:†

" I have not been able to get an authentic statement upon this matter [the citizenship of Riel]; but Hon. Joseph Tasse, M.P., editor *La Minerve,* has written me: ' There cannot be the slightest doubt of the fact that he became an American citizen.' "

Mr. Rambaut could not have made a very thorough investigation. He says:

" Finally he [Riel] settled down as a school-teacher at Sun River, Montana, and in due time became an American citizen."‡

Reference to a postal guide, kept at every postoffice in the United States, would have revealed the fact, to the member of the New York bar, that Sun River is in Lewis and Clarke county, and the further fact, that Helena is the shire town of that county. A letter to the clerk of the United States Court, enclosing one dollar, would have been honoured with a certified copy of the record.

But this author is not distinguished for his accuracy. He says that Riel was hanged on the 10th day of November.§

* Speech in Parliament, delivered March 22, 1886, page 16. † Page 159.
‡ Page 150. § Page 159.

This writer devotes several pages to Riel's case considered from an international stand-point. He says:

"Taking up now the features of the case that have most interest for the student of political science, we notice, in the first place, that although the affidavit of indictment was evidently prepared to meet the objection that Riel was a naturalized American citizen, and therefore no subject of the Queen, the counsel on both sides omitted all reference to this fact. It seems to be generally believed that Riel was naturalized during his residence in the United States If this be true, there can be no doubt that he ceased to be a British subject. The effect of naturalization, long a mooted question between the English and American governments, was definitely settled by the treaty of 1870. Riel was accordingly entitled to the same protection which would be due in like case to a native citizen of the United States. When it became evident that Riel was about to be executed under sentence of the Canadian court, the United States government was asked to interfere in his behalf on account of his American citizenship acquired during his residence in Montana. In this matter, Major Edmond Mallet of Washington, D. C., acted for Riel. He has very kindly written me a letter, in which he succinctly narrates his efforts in Riel's behalf, and the position taken by our government. He says: 'I first consulted Mr Bayard, and he took this position substantially:

"'1. That it was not the duty of the government to inquire into the fact of Riel's American citizenship; and,

"'2. That the government could not interfere even if he was an American citizen, either natural or adopted. If a case was brought to the attention of his department, it would be examined into; but under no circumstances could the government, he thought, interfere unless it was shown conclusively that he had been discriminated against during his trial by reason of his American citizenship.'

"When it became apparent to me that the Canadian government had committed itself to the execution of Riel, under the pressure brought to bear upon it by the Orange lodges of Ontario, I went to the President and appealed to him to prevent this judicial murder. I based my appeal on the following [grounds]:

"1. That Riel was an American citizen; that he had been indicted as a British citizen, his American citizenship having been entirely ignored, although offer had been made to prove the fact by documents captured at the battle of Batoche, and then in the Canadian government's hands; and that he had been tried by a half jury of six men selected by the judge, and that judge was a mere justice of the peace.

"2. That Riel was insane,—and I offered testimony to that effect,—and

"3. That the authority to put a human being to death for any cause whatsoever is not inherent in government, but is delegated from God, and that such delegated power can be exercised only in certain conditions, such as sound mind, etc. The President seemed much interested in the case ; expressed himself in sympathy with what I told him; but he considered it a very grave matter to interfere. At last I asked that he send for Mr. Bayard and the British Minister, and see if an amicable understanding could be made to save Riel. The President then said he would consult with the Secretary of State and see what could be done.

" During the night of the same day the Associated Press announced that the President had been constrained to decline interfering in the matter.

" The position taken by Secretary Bayard rests on sound international law. Our government would not have been justified in interfering in the matter on the basis of the case presented to the Department of State. Although Riel was a naturalized American, he owed the Queen of Great Britain temporary allegiance while living within the borders of her realm, and he made himself liable for breach of the criminal law of the land.   .   .   .   .   .

" Not only had the United States no right to interfere in Riel's behalf, but the Canadian court was in the right in ignoring Riel's citizenship. It was absolutely immaterial."

There is little doubt that there is a kinship between the feelings of Archimedes as he jumped from the bath; of Newton when the idea of his greatest discovery dawned upon his mind; of Columbus as he gazed, for the first time, upon San Salvador, and the feelings of this judicial Columbus at the time this forensic truism first illuminated his cranium, to-wit:

"Although Riel was a naturalized American, he owed the Queen of Great Britain temporary allegiance while living within the borders of her realm, and he made himself liable for breach of the criminal law of the land."*

If this proposition was ever even the subject of serious debate since the foundation of the world, the writer is not aware of it.

Mr. Rambaut states another thing, which is untrue. Edmond Mallet did not appear or act for Riel,† who died in complete ignorance of the fact that any effort, in his behalf, had been made with the President. Major Mallet was a clerk

---

* See pp. 159-161. † It is not meant to convey the idea that Major Mallet made the only effort in Riel's behalf with the government. He made, however, the best presentation of the case.

in the Treasury Department. His communications with the President and Secretary were between a government official and his superiors; and were of a confidential nature. Major Mallet has since been discreetly reticent upon the subject. This is certainty, however: the attention of Grover Cleveland and his prime minister were called to the case and their interference asked, and they declined to act. Comment will be reserved for the close of this volume.

Riel had been thrice respited, by the bevy of moral cowards who composed the cabinet at Ottawa, at cabinet meetings held September 10th, October 22d, and November 10th, respectively. But the preparations for the execution continued, and the day of his doom was at hand.*

Chief Sherwood, of the Dominion Police, arrived at Regina upon a special train the evening of the fifteenth. Colonel Irvine and Sheriff Chapleau entered the doomed man's cell. He anticipated their errand. "You have come with the great announcement," he said. He thanked the sheriff for his kindness, and requested that his body be given to his friends to be buried beside his father at Saint Boniface.

The sheriff asked him if he had any wishes to convey as to the disposition of his personal estate or effects.

"*Mon cher*," replied Riel, "I have only this," touching his breast above the region of the heart. "This I gave to my country fifteen years ago, and it is all I have to give now."

He was asked as to his peace of mind and replied: "I long ago made my peace with my God and am as prepared to die now as I can be at any time."

Pere Andre, his confessor, then arrived.

The sheriff read the death warrant which Sherwood had brought and left the doomed man with his spiritual adviser.

Riel's prison life had set lightly upon him. For years he had been a total abstainer from alcohol and tobacco, and his

---

* The account of Riel's last hours and execution are drawn mostly from the Associated Press dispatches.

diet had been most abstemious. His life-long and proverbial urbanity had not forsaken him in prison. He had given his captors no trouble.

Father Andre was never absent from the doomed man's side, from the reading of the warrant till the fatal drop. They prayed together most fervently till three o'clock, when Riel dozed, and finally slept soundly. In about two hours he awoke, and from that time till eight, when the death-bell began to toll, he prayed almost continuously. At five o'clock mass was said, and at seven the last sacrament was administered.

The scaffold was extended from the rear of the south end of the guard-room. It was twelve minutes past eight before those having tickets from the sheriff were admitted to the room. The prisoner was found kneeling upon the floor of an upper room, from which he was to step to the scaffold. Around him were members of the mounted police, Sheriff Chapleau, Deputy Sheriff Gibson, as well as his spiritual advisers, Fathers Andre and McWilliams. The rays of the early sun shone through the rime which covered the small window. The prisoner knelt beside an open window, which looked out upon the gallows. He wore a loose woolen surtout, flannel shirt, trowsers and moccasins.

Twenty minutes before going to the scaffold Riel wrote the following in French, of which a close translation is given:

" What there is too presumptuous in my writings, I must say that by these presents, I subordinate it entirely to the good pleasure of my God, to the doctrine of the church, and to the infallible decisions of the Supreme Pontiff. I die Catholic, and in the only true faith.

" LOUIS DAVID RIEL.

" 16th Nov., 1885. Regina Jail."

He had before this written a touching letter to his mother, full of filial devotion.

At a quarter past eight the doomed man received the notice to proceed to the scaffold. He mounted the gallows, from which he was never to descend alive, with the firmness of a

Scævola and the resignation of a Socrates. His arms were pinioned before leaving the guard-room. As he walked upon the scaffold, he turned his face from the spectators, and continued praying. Riel rallied his confessor with, "Courage, pere," adressing Father Andre. He was admonished by this priest, to pray for his enemies. He prayed for Sir John A. Macdonald; but added a petition, that Canada might soon be delivered of his reign.

Father McWilliams kissed Riel, who said, "I believe still in God."

"To the last?" asked Father Andre.

"Yes the very last," answered Riel: "I believe and trust in Him. Sacred Heart of Jesus, have mercy upon me."

Dr. Jukes shook hands with the prisoner, who said in English: "Thank you, doctor." Then he continued: "*Jesus, Marie, Joseph, asistez moi en ce dernier moment.*"

When he was about to take his place upon the drop the Deputy Sheriff asked him, if he had anything to say.

"Shall I not say a few words?" he asked of his confessor.

"No," quickly replied the priest, in French; "make this your last sacrifice and you will be rewarded."

Riel then turned and remarked in English, "I have nothing more to say."

The cap was then drawn over his face, and the rope adjusted.

While these things were being done he was given two minutes to pray. He began repeating the *Pater Noster.* At the significant words "*Et ne nos inducas in tentationem.*"* the hangman † sprang the bolt, and the body of the condemned half-breed descended with a terrible crash. The fall of eight

---

* One account says, that Riel's last words were "*Merci, Jesu.*" Another is that he fell while invoking the Saints.

† It was claimed the hangman was one Jack Henderson, who was a prisoner of Riel's at Fort Garry. Begg's book, which purports to give the names of Riel's prisoners, does not mention him. See appendix I.

feet, and the unusual weight of the man dislocated the neck. For a second there was no movement. Then there followed a slight twitching of the muscles; and in two minutes the soul of Louis Riel was in the presence of the Judge of All the Earth.

During the terrible ordeal the colour had not left Riel's face, and there was not the tremour of a muscle. He literally smiled in the face of death.

The body was cut down; the coroner's jury was empaneled by Doctor Dodds, and a verdict of death by hanging rendered. The hair of the deceased was cut off one side of both head and face. All the buttons torn off the coat; the moccasins removed from the feet, and even the suspenders cut into pieces, for persons to obtain mementos of the deceased. He was placed in a plain deal coffin to await the plans of the Government as to interment.

The coffin was then nailed up, to be temporarily placed in the burying-ground attached to the barracks, pending the relatives obtaining permission to carry it to Saint Boniface, where it was afterwards interred.

The account of the execution appended to Mercer Adam's book states, that Riel kept up his courage by praying, thus diverting his thoughts from the terrible death before him. After blistering his mendacious hand in a vain attempt to stamp Riel with the brand of a mercenary and a coward, it is hard for the Canadian to concede to him actual fortitude upon the scaffold. Adam, in this case, credited it to a religion in which he does not himself believe.

Fortitude, in the hour of death, is oftener the result of the inherent power of a human will than the solace of any religion, true or false. Socrates, Sir Thomas More, Bishop Cranmer and Madame Roland met death with equal firmness. These were, respectively Heathen, Catholic, Protestant and Atheist. The pious legends about the death-bed scenes of Paine and Voltaire will not stand the test of investigation.

Danton, about to be guillotined, said: "My dwelling shall soon be in annihilation, but my name shall live in the Pantheon of history." Saint Paul, also about to be beheaded, wrote to Timothy:

"For I am even now ready to be sacrificed : and the time of my dissolution is at hand. I have fought a good fight; I have finished my course; I have kept the faith. For the rest, there is laid up for me a crown of justice, which the Lord, the just Judge, will render to me at that day."

Who is there that, viewing the death of these two men--- that is, the stern stoicism of the philosopher and the sublime faith of the Christian—would not exclaim in the word of Balaam: "Let my soul die the death of the just, and let my last end be like to them."

There was great indignation in Lower Canada at the death of Riel. Sir John A. Macdonald was burned in effigy in Montreal. The infuriated mob committed many acts which, three centuries ago, would have been accounted treason. Latimer and Ridley did not kindle such a fire at Smithfield, as did Riel at Regina.

To pass from the sublime, to something else. Louis Riel, like Louis Kossuth, figured in the degraded world of fashion. The name of the martyr of Regina furnished an advertisement for the hatter; and the "Riel hat" was the fashion in the Province of Quebec. This reminds one of the hero of Austerlitz being left to quarrel with Sir Hudson Lowe.

By far the most interesting view to Americans, is the one taken from an international stand-point.

The facts may be briefly summarized as follows: On the 10th day of October, 1874, Ambrose Lepine was capitally convicted of the murder of Scott, at the Manitoba assizes. Louis Riel, a British subject, having been indicted separately for the same crime, and his principal being convicted, was adjudged to be in contempt in refusing to become amenable to the court; and on the 15th of the same month, a process of outlawry was sued out, and a warrant was issued. On the

12th day of February, 1875, amnesty was granted to Riel on condition of five years' banishment; and forfeiture of political rights. Until this term of banishment was ended Louis Riel refused to become an American citizen. Eight years thereafter, on the sixteenth of March, 1883, he became an American citizen by regular naturalization. In the month of July, 1884, he crossed the International boundary line for the purpose of engaging in a constitutional agitation, in the interests of British subjects, who maintained that they were being deprived of their property-rights in certain lands by the Canadian government, or with the permission of said government. On the 18th day of March, 1884, these people, under the leadership of Louis Riel, abandoned constitutional agitation, and took-up arms to secure their rights. In the suppression of this revolt, fire-arms were used and blood was shed. Three encounters were had with Riel and his followers at Duck Lake, Fish Creek and Batoche, respectively.

The defendant was arraigned upon an information containing six counts. The first three charged, that the prisoner, being a subject of the Queen, made war against Her Majesty at Duck Lake, Fish Creek and Batoche, respectively. The other three, charged that the prisoner, living at the time within the Dominion of Canada and under the Queen's protection, made war against Her Majesty at the same three places. Upon the trial, there was no venue proven. The judge, in his charge, commented upon the evidence, virtually telling the jury how to find. The jury returned a general verdict of guilty. Then followed the judgment and sentence of the court. Upon appeal, the conviction was affirmed. Executive clemency was denied. The government of the United States was asked to interfere, and refused to do so. Riel suffered the capital penalty at Regina, November 16, 1885.

It will be contended herein, that the government should have interfered in the case of Riel.

In describing the duty of the government in a case like

Riel's, the language of President Cleveland himself will be employed:

"The watchful care and interest of this government over its citizens are not relinquished because they are gone abroad, and if charged with a crime committed in the foreign land, a fair and open trial, conducted with a decent regard for justice and humanity, will be demanded for them."[*]

"Out of thy own mouth I judge thee."[†]

Under this rule laid down by the President, it was the duty of his administration to interfere, for the following reasons:

First. Riel was not guilty of any act which could be considered treason, when laying the question of citizenship entirely aside.

Second. Riel was tried upon the theory that he was a citizen of Great Britain; and not of the United States.

Third. The question of the prisoner's sanity or insanity was never fairly submitted to the jury.

Fourth. There was misconduct of the court in instructing the jury.

Fifth. There was a variance between the indictment and the proof:

I. Waiving, for the nonce, the question of citizenship, Riel was yet not guilty of an act amounting to treason. Now, what is treason? Treason, in a general sense, is a "breach of allegiance." In a more restricted sense, it is "any act of hostility against a state, committed by one who owes allegiance to it." The last definition is less accurate than the following: "The offence of attempting to overthrow the government of the state to which the offender owes allegiance, or of betraying the state into the hands of a foreign power." The last definition includes the offence of assassinating the king, or corrupting the queen. For in a monarchical form of government, the king or queen is the personification of legitimate sovereignty.[‡] Consequently, any attempt to take the life of the sovereign, or to corrupt the royal descent is an offence

---

* President Cleveland's message to Congress, December, 1886.   † Luke, xix., 22.   ‡ Guizot's History of Civilization.

against the state itself. The charge of treason, for which Riel was tried and convicted, was that of levying war against Her Majesty in her Realm. This species of treason is founded on a very old statute, passed in the reign of Edward III. The language of that statute is as follows:

"When a man do levy war against our lord the king in his Realm, or he adherent to the king's enemies in his Realm, giving them aid and comfort in the Realm or elsewhere, and thereof be provably attainted of open deed by the people of their condition, that this shall be one ground upon which the party accused of the offence, and legally proven to have committed the offence, shall be held to be guilty of high treason."

The provision of the Constitution of the United States which defines treason, is a substantial copy of the old statute of Edward III. It is as follows: " Treason against the United States shall consist only in levying war against them, or in adhering to their enemies, giving them aid and comfort,"* and-so-forth. The similarity betwixt the English statute and the American constitutional enactment renders the judicial interpretation of the one of value in construing the other. Fortunately for the citizen, but unfortunately for the legal student, the crime of treason has been a stranger to our jurisprudence. The English decisions are of less value because the judges held their positions during the royal pleasure, and royalty was interested in maintaining its prerogative.

The history of the law of treason is but the record of the triumph of liberty over divine right—that bastard cigne of priest-craft and king-craft. Under that abominable despotism which invented the *legem regis*, it was treason to melt down the statue of an emperor, after it was consecrated; it was adjudged treason. In the reign of Edward IV., a landlord, who kept a hotel with the sign of the crown, said he would make his son heir of the crown, intending an innocent pun. For this he was hanged, drawn and quartered; and his prospective heir attainted. In the same reign the king, while hunting, killed a deer. The owner wished the deer's horns

---

*Constitution of the United States, Article III., Section 3.

in the king's stomach. For this offence he suffered death. In the reign of the great "reformer," Henry VIII., it was declared to be treason for a person to believe the king's marriage with Anne of Cleves to be legal and valid. Where there were two rivals for the throne the unsuccessful partisans suffered death.

Judge Brackenridge says, that, during the contest between the houses of Lancaster and York, England was, for years, nothing but a Golgotha. The definition of treason is what Macaulay says of the habeas corpus act—"one of the most stringent checks which legislation ever imposed on tyranny."[*] It is the only definition found in our fundamental law. The fact is significant of the fear which our fathers had for this dangerous plaything of tyrants.

There are two offences which superficial and illogical reasoners are apt to confound. These are treason and riot. Riot is defined thus: " A tumultuous disturbance of the peace, by three persons or more, assembling together of their own authority with an intent mutually to assist one another, against any one who shall oppose them, in the execution of some enterprise of a private nature; and afterwards actually executing the same in a violent and turbulent manner, to the terror of the people, whether the act intended were lawful or unlawful."[†]

Treason has already been defined. It differs from riot in this: the object of the traitorous proceedings must be of a public, and not a private nature; in the particular species of treason charged against Riel, there must be a levying of war. There may be an assembly of armed men, who may be furnished with guns, rifles, pistols, bayonets and other weapons; they may forcibly resist the conservators of the peace and proceed to the last extremity. But still, unless the object of the assembly be of a public or general nature, there is no treason. The two offences of treason and riot have so many

---

[*] History of England, Vol. 1.   [†] Bouvier, Bishop, Wharton.

ingredients in common, that one is often mistaken for the other.
We often read of people assembling together; breaking open
a jail, and resisting the authority of the sheriff, for the purpose of lynching some obnoxious criminal. But this is not
levying war. In the year 1863, several thousand of the inhabitants of New York City arose in a body in resistance of
conscription; they murdered negroes; burned an orphan asylum, and nearly ruined the *Tribune* office. Yet no one ever
dreamt of accusing these men of treason. More than a quarter
of a century ago, the citizens of California organized themselves
into vigilance committees; and forcibly assumed the functions
of the courts. But this was not levying war. If such forced
constructions as have governed the English courts prevailed,
there would be little safety for the subject. Such cramped
and far-fetched constructions might convict any man of treason. When a child, I listened to the following logic from the
chairman of the school-board, who was addressing the scholars:
" If you resist your teacher, you resist me; if you resist me,
you resist the sheriff; if you resist the sheriff, you resist the
militia of the state."* Is the child who rebels against the
teacher guilty of constructive treason? In this state, a few
years ago, the people of certain counties organized themselves
into bands for the alleged purpose of protecting their property, but for the practical purpose of hanging men accused of
horse-stealing. These men had been obliged to sleep in their
horse-barns for years, to prevent their animals from being
stolen. This became monotonous; they thought the government was insufficient; and they took the law in their own
hands. Without discussing the wisdom or policy of this
course, I think no lawyer would risk his reputation in an effort
to obtain a conviction of treason against those men. It was
held by five judges, that a rise of all the weavers in and about
London, for the purpose of destroying all engine-looms was
not treason. What then is the gravamen of the offence

* Edward D. Rand, of Lisbon, N. H., afterwards Circuit Judge.

of treason? It is that which must be the essential ingredient of every felony and every misdemeanor, except, perhaps, nuisance, to-wit: the criminal intent developed in a direct attempt to commit the particular offence charged. Judge Brackenridge, the Blackstone of Pennsylvania, says upon this subject:

"I would in the first place lay aside constructive treasons altogether, and confine the law to a direct attack upon the government, and in the second place I would confine it to an attack, *animi subvertendi*. Will it not be easy then to meditate the overthrowing the government, and go on to execute it by a resistance to a law, and by risings for indirect purposes, without a possibility of making proof of an *animus subvertendi*, or conspiracy to overthrow? Let it be left to the jury to presume, or infer from the acts themselves, what the intention was; but let it always be in view as the essence of the act, that there was a directly looking forward in the mind of the person to a subversion of the government, before it be constructed treason. Every outrage, without this essential ingredient may be repressed and punished under the idea of a riot, subjecting to fine, pillory, imprisonment, and hard labour. This will be more agreeable to the common sense and feelings of mankind, who must be struck with a sense that the outrage is a riot, but to whom it cannot be obvious that it was meditated as an attempt upon the government itself, amounting to high treason. It is only by deduction and inference, that it becomes so."*

The reader will remember that the Saskatchewan rebellion was local only, and according to Lord Melgund, the insurgents only sought to defend their homes against invasion.†

Why should Riel and his followers be held guilty of treason for protecting themselves against land-thieves more than the "vigilantes" of Nebraska, who were defending their property against the notorious Albert Wade and his gang of horse-thieves? Is the difference between real estate and personal property at the bottom of the distinction? At common law, a man who picked apples from his neighbour's trees without his permission was guilty of a simple trespass; while he who picked a windfall from the ground without leave was a thief, because the apple on the tree was attached to the realty.

* Law Miscellanies, page 495. † Recent Rebellion in the North-West, *Nineteenth Century*, August, 1885.

Here now comes another curious novelty of law: The man who steps outside law to defend his horse is guilty of riot, assault or, at worst, of murder. But he who steps outside the law to defend his home is guilty of treason. Why? Because his horse is personal property, and his home is real estate. Profundity of logic! There was once an astute mathematician who tried to prove that the sum of the angles of an isosceles triangle were equal to two right angles by the music of the spheres. There is a great weight of authorities (English) against the author's position. He agrees with Brackenridge. The opinions of judges are not the law. They are simply the evidences of the law.

The only evidence that Riel intended anything amounting to high treason was the wild statements made by him, as testified to by Doctor John H. Willoughby and others. Here follows a portion of Willoughby's testimony:

"Q. Go on? A. He [Riel] made a statement as to my knowledge of his rebellion, that is of the former rebellion in 1870, and he said that he was an American citizen, living in Montana, and that the half-breeds had sent a deputation there to bring him to this country.

"Q. What else? A. That in asking him to come they had told him their plans, and he had replied to them to the effect that their plans were useless.

"Q. Did he say what the plans were? A. No, I believe not, but that he had told them that he had plans, and that if they would assist him to carry out those plans he would go with them.

"Q. Did he tell you what those plans were? A. Yes, he did.*

"Q. What were they? A. He said the time had now come when those plans were mature; that his proclamation was at Pembina, and that as soon as he struck the first blow here, that proclamation would go forth and he was to be joined by

---

* A contradiction.

half-breeds and Indians, and that the United States was at his back.

"Q. Did he tell you anything more? A. He said that knowing him and his past history, I might know that he meant what he said.

"Q. Anything else? A. He said that the time had come now when he was to rule this country or perish in the attempt.

"Q. Go on? A. We had a long conversation then as to the rights of the half-breeds, and he laid-out his plans as to the government of the country.

"Q. What did he say as to the government of the country? A. They were to have a new government in the North-West. It was to be composed of God-fearing men. They would have no such Parliament as the House at Ottawa.

"Q. Anything else? A. Then he stated how he intended to divide the country into seven portions.

"Q. In what manner? A. It was to be divided into seven portions, but as to who were to have the seven, I can not say.

"Q. You mean to say you can not say how these seven were to be apportioned? A. Yes, he mentioned Bavarians, Poles, Italians, Germans, Irish. There was to be a new Ireland in the North-West.

"Q. Anything more? Did he say anything more about himself or his own plans? A. I recollect nothing further, at the present time.

"Q. You say he referred to the previous rebellion of 1870. What did he say in regard to that? A. He referred to that and he said that that rebellion—the rebellion of fifteen years ago—would not be a patch upon this one."

Any man who will believe that Riel ever uttered this language, or, if he did, was serious in its utterance, must discredit Riel's sanity. Such language, too, was inconsistent with his subsequent conduct, and that of the half-breeds.

The reader will bear in mind, that the author is not the
9

first person to suggest these ideas. The Honourable William Macdougall, whose ability as a constitutional lawyer is certainly worthy of recognition, was reported as saying, that there had been no evidence produced to show that Riel's intention was to depose the Queen. On the contrary, he said, that General Middleton had reported to the government, that he discovered Riel's intention was to take him prisoner, and hold him until the government granted the half-breeds their demands as to lands. This was positive proof, that Riel had no intention and made no demands against the Crown, which alone could constitute high treason. It appears, that the privy council in England in giving judgment in the case, assumed that this fact had been admitted by Riel's counsel at the time of the trial. Riel's action, said Mr. Macdougall, was simply a riot, started in the hope that the government would be led to accord the half-breeds their rights.*

If wrong, the author is content to " err with Plato."

11. Next, Riel was tried upon the theory, that he was a citizen of Great Britain, and not of the United States. As before stated, the question of his citizenship was totally ignored, after the motion for a continuance was disposed-of.

Thomas D. Rambaut, " Ph. D.," says, that the question was wholly immaterial: In the words of Saint Augustine, " *Roma locuta, causa finita.*" †

It is true that treason can be committed by an alien, who is a mere denizen, or a person within the jurisdiction of the sovereignty, the only exception which is called to mind, being in the case of foreign ambassadors, and alien enemies invading the country. These first, by fiction of law, are considered as being within the jurisdiction of the sovereignty from which they are accredited. The second are but the servants of the sovereignty to which they owe allegiance.

So far as the capability to commit the offence of treason is

---

* *Chicago Times*, November 11, 1885.   Military report of General Middleton.
† Rome hath spoken, the case is finished.

concerned, the question of citizenship is, perhaps, immaterial. But there is this distinction: the allegiance of the resident alien is temporary; and only continues while he is domiciled within the country. But the allegiance of the citizen is perpetual, unless he expatriate himself, and attaches to him wherever he may be, whether in the sands of Sahara or in the snows of Siberia.

In all indictments for treason the allegation of venue, as in the information against Riel, is a customary allegation: "At the locality known as Fish Creek, in the said North-West Territories of Canada, and within this Realm," and-so-forth. Probably if the fact of the offender's citizenship appeared, the venue would not be material.

But, in a case involving life or limb, a fact material to the establishment of the gravamen or gist of the offence can hardly be presumed against the defendant. It would seem, that either the citizenship or the venue would have to be established as a matter of proof. The latter, being the most salient point of such proof, would be the easy and natural one.

There is not in the whole record of Riel's trial, one jot or tittle of proof, that he committed a single overt act within the Realm of Her Britannic Majesty. No lawyer will claim, that a court could take judicial cognizance of the fact, that a wild stream running through a ravine was within the venue laid in the indictment. The lawyers who tried the cause at Regina were not fools, and the only rational presumption is, that they were proceeding upon the assumption, that Riel was a citizen of Canada.

It can not be contended that the Dominion government proceeded upon the theory of "once a citizen, always a citizen." For this relic of feudalism is, long since, exploded. The right of expatriation, so long contended for by America, was conceded by Great Britain in the treaty of 1870.* It has been acknowledged by the nations of continental Europe since the French Revolution.†

* Porter Morse on Citizenship.   † Ibid.

It may be contended on behalf of President Cleveland, that, as Riel's counsel never urged the question of his citizenship at the trial, and as he never himself petitioned the United States government, the government was justified in refusing to even examine into the question of his naturalization. This is too absurd for serious refutation. Such a rule would have left Martin Koszta to imprisonment and death. If the Greeks of Homer had acted upon such a theory, they would have been deaf to the "groans and cries of Helen."

III. The point as to Riel's insanity was never fairly submitted to the jury. He was tried under the old rule, which prevailed in England, that upon the question of sanity or insanity, the burden is upon the defendant. This is the rule which prevails in most of the states of the American Union; and there is nothing particularly cruel about it.

It was shown, that Riel had once been insane. There can be no doubt upon this point. He was afflicted with a most peculiarly deceptive form of insanity. It further appeared, that, at the time of the commission of the acts complained-of, the defendant exhibited the same symptoms which were discovered at the period of his former affliction.

Such a state of facts established, the most careful and painstaking inquiry was demanded; the thorough sifting of the facts, and the scrupulous weighing of the proofs. The only witness whose testimony was of any value was Doctor Roy. He unhesitatingly pronounced Riel insane. The others had only a few hours' examination upon which to base an opinion which it required months to form with any degree of certainty. After the verdict, the government sought to bolster it up with a batch of *ex-parte* certificates. It is needless to write upon the value of *ex-parte* testimony, even where the witness is under oath. Cross-examination, as every lawyer knows, is the great discoverer of falsehood.

IV. The misconduct of the court, in commenting upon the

testimony, has already been spoken of, in the account of the trial.*

V. There was a material variance between the information and the proofs.

Each count of the information, upon which Riel was condemned, contained the following allegation: "Together with divers false traitors, to the said Alexander David Stewart unknown," and-so-forth.

Upon this method of pleading, that is, describing a person in an indictment as unknown, Mr. Bishop says:

"Suppose it turns out on the evidence that the grand jury were wilfully ignorant, and might have known the name if they had chosen; then, the reason on which this form of the allegation is allowed, failing, the allegation itself will be held on the trial to be insufficient, or to be insufficiently sustained by the proofs adduced. As observed in an English case, 'The want of description is only excused when the name cannot be known.' In other words, since the doctrine which allows this form of the allegation rests on necessity, it can be sustained no further than its foundation extends."†

This certainly would be necessary in a trial for high treason, a crime which, as every lawyer knows, is, like riot and conspiracy, impossible for one man to commit alone. It is impossible to believe that Alexander David Stewart had not heard of Gabriel Dumont and other half-breeds engaged with Riel. The variance was fatal.

In speaking of President Cleveland, the writer will be mindful of the facts, that that man is, at present, the representative of over fifty millions of people; that the citizens who have chosen him as their standard-bearer, are the author's countrymen; and constitute, presumably, one of the most enlightened nations under heaven; that before being called to this high position, he had been Governor of the great state of New York, receiving, upon his election to that office, the largest relative, if not absolute majority, of any candidate in the history of our country; that when elected to the presidential chair, Mr. Cleveland was an un-

---

* Page 110, this volume. † Criminal Procedure, Vol. I., page 335.

known man, whose demise would hardly have caused a local sensation, while his opponent was a man really illustrious; that when elected president his competitor was one of the most famous men in America, with large experience in public affairs.

In commenting upon the official conduct of the Secretary of State, the writer will try to bury personal prejudice, and forget, that it was Thomas F. Bayard who said, that Philip H. Sheridan was unfit to breathe the free air of a republic.

"Thou shalt not speak evil of the prince of thy people," is the writer's scriptural motto.

An ancient sage was once asked what was the best form of government. He answered, in substance, that that form of government was the best which treated an injury to the meanest citizen as a wrong to the state itself. A more accurate definition could not be framed.

The excellence of a government is in its substance and not its form. A demagogue elevated to power by an ignorant and clamouring mob, is hardly preferable to the despot ruling by the ancient fiction of divine right.

The pages of the Pentateuch and Iliad, as well as the columns of the modern newspaper, bear testimony to the willingness of a good government to protect the rights of its citizens.

At the time of the expedition of the four kings, Lot, the nephew of Abraham, was taken prisoner. In those patriarchal days the family was the state. The story is told in the XIV. chapter of Genesis, and it is impossible to improve upon the simplicity of the sacred narrative:

"When Abram had heard, to-wit, that his brother Lot was taken, he numbered of the servants born in his house, three hundred and eighteen well appointed: and pursued them to Dan. And dividing his company, he rushed upon them in the night, and defeated them, and pursued them as far as Hobah, which is on the left hand of Damascus. And he brought back all the substance, and Lot his brother with his substance, the women also and the people. And the King of Sodom went out to meet him after he returned from the slaughter of Chodorlahomor, and of the kings that were with him in the vale of Save, which is the King's vale. But Melchisedech, the King of Salem, bringing forth bread and wine, for he was the Priest of the most high God, blessed him, and said : Blessed be Abram by the most high God, who created heaven and earth. And blessed be the most high God, by whose protection the enemies are in thy hands. And he gave him the tithes of all. And the King of Sodom said to Abram : Give me the persons and the rest take to thyself. And he answered him : I lift up my hand to the Lord God, the most high, the possessor of heaven and earth, that from the very woof-thread unto the shoe-latchet, I will not take of any things that are thine, lest thou say : I have enriched Abram: except such things as the young men have eaten, and the shares of the men that came with me, Aner, Escol and Mambre: these shall take their shares."

The Mesopotamian considered an injury done to one of his kin as an injury to the patriarchal state itself.

Paul was apprehended upon the charge of sedition and sacrilege. He was bound with thongs, and the torturer's lash was about to be administered, when the intimation that the prisoner was a Roman citizen stayed the uplifted hand. The words: *Civis Romanus sum*, had such power that even a poor tent-maker, in an obscure province of the Roman Empire, could, by their single utterance, save himself from the ignominious discipline of the scourge.

An insult to the humblest of Rome's citizens was a wrong to the Empire itself.

Turning from scriptural to classic tale, we read of the story of the Grecian Helen, carried off by Paris, the libertine prince of Troy. This rape of Helen was considered, by the whole Achaian race, as an insult, not only to Sparta, whose queen she was, but to Thessalians and Epirots and Argives alike. The Greeks fitted out an array of 1,200 vessels, and 100,000 men.

This great fleet set sail; but the first time they mistook a part of the Asiatic coast called Teuthrania, for the plains of Troy; and, a storm arising, they were driven back upon the Grecian coast. The scattered fleet was collected at Aulis, upon the coast of Greece. Agamemnon, according to the legend, is informed, that the expedition cannot proceed unless his daugher Iphigenia is sacrificed to the gods. So sacred were the rights of a Grecian, that a virgin's blood was not too dear a price to be paid for the ransom of the captive princess. Better the death of one woman than the dishonour of another.

An injury done to a frail woman was an insult, not only to her nation, but to the entire race.

In the year 1847 there lived at Athens a Portuguese Jew, named Don Pacifico. This man was a native of Gibraltar, hence, by accident, a native-born subject of her Britannic Majesty. It had been customary amongst the Greeks to celebrate Easter by burning an effigy of Judas Iscariot. But that year the police had been commanded to prevent it. The disappointed rabble charged this to the secret influence of the Jews. Poor Don Pacifico happened to live near the spot where the imaginary Judas was annually burned. The unfortunate Hebrew, being the handiest thing, was selected by the mob as the devoted object of their wrath. Don Pacifico claimed an indemnity of nearly thirty-two thousand pounds. Lord Palmerston was at the head of the foreign office. He demanded an immediate settlement. Palmerston became possessed of the idea that the French government was interfering against the claim of Don Pacifico. This nearly involved England in a war with France. Finally Sir William Parker was ordered to Athens for the purpose of obtaining satisfaction. Failing in this, the Admiral blockaded the Piraeus. The Greek government appealed to France and Russia, as powers joined with England in a treaty to protect the independence of Greece. The powers complained that they had not been consulted in the affair, when they were told, in diplomatic language, to mind their own business. During this controversy Lord Stanley introduced resolutions of censure upon the ministry. They were carried in the Upper House. Mr. Roebuck introduced a contrary resolution in the Lower House. This led to one of the most remarkable debates on record, in which Sir Alexander Cockburn made his reputation in support of Palmerston. The minister triumphed, and the right of a despised Israelite to the protection of the flag under which he was born was established.

Thus was an injury to a Portuguese Jew (surely not better than an educated half-breed) considered an insult to the honour of a Christian state.

In the year 1864, Theodore, the King of Abyssinia, imprisoned Captain Cameron, a citizen of Great Britain. Two years later he was released on the demand of the foreign office; but was again remanded to prison. A second demand from the Queen met with no response. The British government fitted-out, at Bombay, an army of 4,000 English troops and 8,000 sepoys under Sir Robert Napier. They landed at Annelsey Bay. They marched through the pass of Senafe, and through four hundred miles of desert waste and proceeded to Magdala. They stormed that mountain fortress, set their captive countryman at liberty; and "planted the standard of Saint George on the mountains of Rasselas."*

All this for the release of an obscure subject whose name would have been unknown to fame, but for the fact, that his Queen deemed his imprisonment an insult to Her Majesty.

Who of us Americans has not felt his heart swell with pride at the tale of Martin Koszta† and Captain Ingraham. We can almost forgive Duncan Ingraham for his subsequent treason, in view of his plucky conduct at Smyrna. The tale is familiar to every school-boy.

Kostza was a Hungarian who had been engaged in the rebellion of 1848. Subsequently, in New York, he had declared his intention of becoming an American citizen. He afterwards went to Smyrna, where he was seized by some persons in the employment of the Austrian consul. Koszta

---

* Disraeli's speech in Parliament upon the elevation of Sir Robert Napier to the peerage, as Baron Napier of Magdala.   † Porter Morse on Citizenship, pp. 68-70, 108, 244.

was taken out into the harbour, and thrown overboard.   He was picked up by an Austrian man-of-war, and held a prisoner.   The United States consul remonstrated in vain.

The United States sloop-of-war Saint Louis, Captain Duncan N. Ingraham was in the harbour.   The chivalrous commander instantly demanded Koszta's release.   Upon being refused, he cleared his vessel for action, when the Austrian commander deemed it prudent to yield.   Koszta was given up; and shipped to the United States.   William L. Marcy, the then Secretary of State, under President Pierce, sustained Captain Ingraham's action, in a diplomatic correspondence with M. Hulseman, the *charge d'affaires* of Austria.

We had a government then.   Let it be remembered that Koszta had fled a fugitive from Austria; and while under ban, he had simply declared his intention of becoming an American citizen.   Yet so jealous was Pierce's administration of the rights of Americans, that an injury done to one who only intended to become an American citizen was a wrong to the state itself.

Mr. Blaine, while Secretary of State, refused to allow a certificate of naturalization from an American court to be even questioned in a proceeding upon the arbitration of a claim to indemnity for injury done to the property of an American citizen in Cuba.*   This position was thought to be an extreme and an illegal one.   But better, a thousand to one, such an error than the crime of allowing an American citizen to be hanged almost in sight of our border.

The inconsistency of the foreign policy of the present administration is discerned by a comparison between the case of Louis Riel and that of Augustus K. Cutting.†

Cutting was a strolling renegade; a homeless, houseless vagabond.   He followed the business of a printer, and belonged to a class with which every one is acquainted—miserable

---

* *In re* Buzzi *against* Spain.   † Foreign Relations of the United States, 1886, pp. 691–708.

leeches, who frequent small towns and, calling themselves editors, eke out a precarious existence by levying blackmail upon respectable citizens, and periodically nauseating the public taste with printed sheets full of false syntax, poor orthography and worse typography.

This man was living at Paso del Norte, Mexico, a place famous as being, for a long time, the seat of the Juarez government; the spot where that noble patriot made his last stand, and refused to abandon Mexican soil.

A gentleman, by the name of Emigdio Medina, purposed starting another newspaper in the same town, which he had a right to do. For this crime Cutting abused him through the columns of his paper, *El Centinela*. For this libel Cutting was brought before the Mexican court. Under the law when the parties agree to and sign a reconciliation the case is dismissed, which was done in this instance, Mr. Cutting being required by the court to publish it in his paper, which he did.

On the 18th day of June, 1886, Cutting crossed the river to El Paso, Texas, and published the following disgusting piece of solecism in the *El Paso Herald:*

"ADVERTISEMENT.—A CARD."

"EL PASO, TEX., *June 18, 1886.*

" *To Emigdio Medina, of Paso del Norte:*

"In a late issue of *El Centinela*, published in Paso del Norte, Mexico, I made the assertion that Emigdio Medina was a 'fraud,' and that the Spanish newspaper he proposed to issue in Paso del Norte was a scheme to swindle advertisers, etc. This morning said Medina took the matter to a Mexican court, where I was forced to sign a 'reconciliation.'

"Now, I do hereby reiterate my original assertion, that said Emigdio Medina is a 'fraud,' and add 'dead-beat' to the same. Also, that his taking advantage of the Mexican law and forcing me to a 'reconciliation' was *contemptible* and *cowardly* and in keeping with the odorous reputation of said Emigdio Medina. And should said Emigdio Medina desire 'American' satisfaction for this reiteration, I will be pleased to grant him all he may desire, at any time, in any manner." "A. K. CUTTING."

The libel was circulated in El Paso del Norte, on the Mexican side of the river. For this offence Cutting was arrested.

He was first charged under a law, peculiar to Mexico, which presumes to mete out justice for offences against Mexican citizens committed on a foreign soil. But the complaint was afterwards amended to include the publication of the libel in Mexico. So the charge was then similar in the nature of its duplicity to that preferred against Riel.

The history of the disgusting nonsense which followed is familiar to the world. Our government incurred thousands of dollars of useless expense in behalf of a gipsy printer who got no more than his deserts. Sedgwick, the disciple of Bacchus, was sent to Mexico to impress Mexicans with the idea that himself and Cutting were specimens of American manhood. The president made Cutting's case a subject of special mention in his message to Congress. But the whole affair ended without a single concession on the part of Mexico.

Contrast the two: Riel, who refused to become an American citizen while he was under the sentence of banishment, was not deemed worthy of even having the question of his citizenship investigated. While Cutting, who sneaked behind his American citizenship to protect himself in the commission of a crime, was worthy of the most Herculean efforts of our government in his behalf.

The reader will recall the fact that on the 19th day of June, 1867, Maximilian was shot at Queretaro. His doom was just. Maximilian was nothing but a common land-pirate. By the infamous Black Decree of October 3, 1865, he repealed the laws of civilized warfare. It treated the republicans as bandits and allowed of no appeal. No record of the transaction was made, except the execution. The shooting of Thomas Scott, viewed from an Orangeman's stand-point, pales into tender mercy beside the wholesale butchery of the Austrian. The instrument of this cruelty was Leonard Marquez, the perpetrator of the massacre of Tacubaya. The name of this bloodthirsty wretch should be written with those of Caligula and Ivan the Terrible.

Yet when Maximilian was shot a wail of pity went from this broad land. " Poor Carlotta! " was upon every tongue. And why was this? Maximilian was a prince. He was, with one exception, the relative of every crowned head in Europe; cousin to Victoria, and brother to Francis Joseph. We Americans are not rid of that damnable fiction of priest-craft and king-craft. " Whatever pleases the Prince is right." In Rome it was called *lex regis;* in Russia they call it "divine right."

If Maximilian had a wife, so had Riel. Carlotta went mad; Riel's wife, upon hearing the verdict, fled to the wilderness, and with difficulty was brought back, and after his death followed him to the grave, dying of a broken heart.

Riel deserved the sympathy of all freemen, but did not receive it. Maximilian merited his doom, but was the object of undeserved pity.

This little book is not written with the expectation that President Cleveland will ever read it, or, if he did, that he would ever comprehend it. Cleveland is called a man of destiny. He has met, in his life, with a single misfortune. It was his defeat for the office of County Attorney of Erie county. Had he been elected to that office, he might have learned sufficient law to have understood that, in a criminal case, the venue is a very material part of the proof and indispensible to a conviction.

It is the boast of this republic that all men are free and equal; that the most lowly born among us can aspire to superlative political honours. We declaim of the Mill-Boy of the Slashes, and of the Illinois rail-splitter, who landed in the White House. But Clay and Lincoln were men who had been schooled by long experience in public affairs. The career of each of these men is as the growth of the oak, not the rise of the rocket.

Josephus tells a tale which carries its moral with it. It is an account of the election of the last of the high priests.

The glory had departed from Jerusalem; and Ichabod was written upon her walls. The account is the sad story of the degradation of a people:

"Hereupon they sent for one of the pontifical tribes, which is called Eniachim and cast lots which of it should be the high priest. By fortune, the lot so fell as to demonstrate their iniquity after the plainest manner, for it fell upon one whose name was Phannias, the son of Samuel, of the village Aphtha. He was a man not only unworthy of the high-priesthood, but that did not know well what high-priesthood was: such a mere rustic was he! Yet did they hail this man, without his own consent, out of the country, as if they were acting a play upon the stage, and adorned him with a counterfeit face; they also put upon him the sacred garments, and upon every occasion instructed him what he was to do. This horrid piece of wickedness was sport and pastime with them, but occasioned the other priests, who at a distance saw their law made a jest of, to shed tears and sorely lament the dissolution of such a sacred dignity."*

There is an old proverb: "Put a beggar on horseback, and unto the devil he will ride."

---

* Wars of the Jews, Book IV., Chapter III.

NONDUM FINIS.

APPENDICES.

APPENDIX A.

———

ACKNOWLEDGMENTS.

———

I CONFESS myself under obligations to the following named gentlemen for valuable aid and assistance in the completion of this work:

FOR PUBLIC DOCUMENTS.

To Honourable CHARLES H. VAN WYCK, Nebraska City; Honourable CHARLES F. MANDERSON, Omaha, Nebraska; to my townsman, Honourable EDWARD K. VALENTINE; GEORGE W. BURBRIDGE, Sir FREDERICK D. MIDDLETON and BENJAMIN SULTE of Ottawa, Canada; Honourable EDWARD BLAKE and JAMES BAINE & SON, of Toronto, Canada.

FOR FACTS.

To Sir FREDERICK D. MIDDLETON, before named; Honourable HUGH RICHARDSON, of Regina; JOSEPH RIEL, brother of LOUIS, who writes from Saint Vital, Manitoba; The Most Reverend ALEXANDER ANTONIN TACHE, Archbishop of Saint Boniface, and Father ERNSTER, the assistant of my friend and pastor, the Reverend JOSEPH RUESING, pastor of Saint Mary's church, West Point.

For kind words and valuable typographical suggestions: To my friend, GRANT NELIGH, of this city.

I must not forget my little amanuensis, ZED BRIGGS.

10

I have read the following books, pamphlets and papers:

The Creation of Manitoba, or History of the Red River Troubles, by ALEXANDER BEGG.

ADAM, G. MERCER. The North-West: Its History and Its Troubles. Toronto, 1885.

Canadian Public Documents. The Queen *vs.* Louis Riel. Ottawa, 1886.

Rebellion in North-West Canada, *The Nineteenth Century*, August, 1885.

MULVANEY, CHARLES PELHAM. History of the North-West Rebellion. Toronto, 1885.

RUNDALL, THOMAS. Voyages toward the North-West, 1496 to 1631. Hakluyt Society Publication. Statutes, Papers, and Canadian Public Documents.

Beside the foregoing, I have consulted the files of various newspapers of Canada and of the United States.

I have read:

Rebellion Number of the *Winnipeg Sun.*

Speech of Honourable EDWARD BLAKE, delivered in House of Commons at Ottawa, March, 1886.

Speech of Honourable JOHN S. D. THOMPSON, delivered in the House of Commons.

Manitoba ; Its Infancy, Growth, and Present Condition, Professor BRYCE.

Campaign speeches of Honourable EDWARD BLAKE, published in pamphlet form: Hunter, Rose & Co., Toronto.

THOMAS D. RAMBAUT's book, and others too numerous to mention.

Professor GOODRICH, of Burlington, Vt., has the thanks of his old pupil for critical suggestions.

I have other sources of information, that I do not feel at liberty to disclose.

W. F. B.

WEST POINT, *1887.*

APPENDIX B.

———

[*Indictment upon Which Riel Was Outlawed.*]

———

HONI SOIT QUI MAL Y PENSE. DIEU ET MON DROIT.

———

CANADA, } Court of Queen's Bench. (Crown Side.)
PROVINCE OF MANITOBA. }

———

NOVEMBER TERM, 1873.

———

THE jurors for our Lady the Queen, upon their oath, present:

That Louis Riel, on the fourth day of March, in the year of our Lord one thousand eight hundred and seventy, at Upper Fort Garry, a place then known as being and lying and situate in the district of Assinniboia, in the Red River settlement, in Rupert's Land, and now known as being, lying and situate at Winnipeg, in the county of Selkirk, in the Province of Manitoba, Dominion of Canada, feloniously, wilfully and of his malice aforethought, did kill and murder one Thomas Scott.*

Against the form of the statute, in such case made and pro-

———

* It is unnecessary to point out to a criminal lawyer, that the charging part of this indictment is good for nothing. Under such pleading, a man might be convicted of shooting, stabbing or poisoning, and-so-on, *ad infinitum.*

vided, and against the peace of our said Lady the Queen, her Crown and dignity.

[Signed]   HENRY J. CLARKE, Q.C.,
                                          Attorney-General.

————

[*Indorsed as Follows:*]

No. 18. Court of Queen's Bench (Crown side), Manitoba. November Term, 1873.   The Queen *against* Louis Riel. Indictment for murder.   A true bill.

[Signed]   W. S. LANSDALE,
                                              Foreman.

————

Fyled this 15th November, 1873.   Judgment of outlawry this 10th day of February, A.D. 1875.

[Signed]   DANIEL CASEY,
                      Prothonotary and Clerk of Crown and Peace.

APPENDIX C.

[*Copy of the Record of Riel's Naturalization.*]

IN THE U. S. DISTRICT COURT OF THE THIRD JUDICIAL DISTRICT OF THE TERRITORY OF MONTANA.

PRESENT: HON. D. S. WADE, JUDGE.

IN THE MATTER OF THE APPLICATION OF LOUIS DAVID RIEL, AN ALIEN, To BECOME A CITIZEN OF THE UNITED STATES OF AMERICA.	*IN OPEN COURT,* *March Term, A.D. 1883,* *this 16th day of March, A.D. 1883, as yet of said Term.*

IT appearing to the satisfaction of this court, by the oaths of E. L. Merrill and Levi Jerome, citizens of the United States of America, witnesses for that purpose; first duly sworn and examined, that Louis David Riel, a native of Canada, has resided within the limits and under the jurisdiction of the United States five years at least, last past, and within the Territory of Montana for one year last past; and that during all of said five years' time he has behaved as a man of good moral character, attached to the principles of the Constitution of the United States, and well disposed to the good order and happiness of the same; and it also appearing to the Court, by competent evidence, that the said applicant has heretofore, and more than two years since, and in due form of law, declared his intention to become a citizen of the United States, and having now here, before this Court, taken an oath that he will support the Constitution of the United States of America, and that he doth absolutely and entirely renounce and abjure all allegiance and fidelity to every foreign Prince, Potentate, State or Sovereignty whatever, and particularly to Victoria, Queen of Great Britain. It is therefore ordered, adjudged and decreed, that the said Louis David Riel be and he is hereby admitted and declared to be a citizen of the United States of America.

D. S. WADE,
Judge.

SIGNATURE: LOUIS DAVID RIEL.

OFFICE OF THE CLERK OF THE UNITED
   STATES DISTRICT COURT OF THE THIRD
   JUDICIAL DISTRICT OF THE TERRITORY } ss.
   OF MONTANA.

I, B. K. Tatem, Clerk of the United States District Court of the Third Judicial District of the Territory of Montana, said court being a court of record, having common law jurisdiction, and a Clerk and Seal, do certify that the above is a true copy of the Act of Naturalization of Louis David Riel as the same appears upon the records of said court now in my office.

In testimony whereof, I have hereunto set my hand and affixed the seal of the said court this 9th day of [L.S.] October, in the year of our Lord one thousand eight hundred and eighty-six, and in the year of our Independence the 111th.

B. K. TATEM,
Clerk.

By C. G. REYNOLDS, *Deputy Clerk.*

APPENDIX D.

— — —

[*Information upon Which Riel was Tried, Convicted and Executed.*]

— — —

SIXTH day of July, in the year of our Lord 1885, at the town of Regina, in the North-West Territories.

Before me, Hugh Richardson, one of the Stipendiary Magistrates, of the North-West Territories, exercising criminal jurisdiction under the provisions of the North-West Act, 1880.

Louis Riel, you stand charged on oath before me, as follows:

" The information and complaint of Alexander David Stewart, of the city of Hamilton, in the Province of Ontario, in the Dominion of Canada, chief of police, taken the sixth day of July, in the year of our Lord one thousand eight hundred and eighty-five, before the undersigned, one of Her Majesty's Stipendiary Magistrates, in and for the said North-West Territories of Canada, who saith:

" 1. That Louis Riel being a *subject of Our Lady the Queen**, not regarding the duty of allegiance, nor having the fear of God in his heart, but being moved and seduced by the instigation of the devil, as a false traitor against our said Lady the Queen, and wholly withdrawing the allegiance, fidelity and obedience which every true and faithful subject of our said Lady the Queen, should and of right ought to bear towards our said Lady the Queen, in the year aforesaid, on the twenty-sixth day of March, together with divers other false traitors, to the said Alexander David Stewart unknown, armed and arrayed in a warlike manner, that is to say, with

---

* The *Italics* are mine.

guns, rifles, pistols, bayonets and other weapons, being then unlawfully, maliciously and traitorously assembled and gathered together against our said Lady the Queen, at the locality known as Duck Lake, in the said the North-West Territories of Canada, and within this Realm, and did then maliciously and traitorously attempt and endeavour by force and arms to subvert and destroy the constitution and government of this Realm, as by law established, and deprive and depose our said Lady the Queen of and from the style, honour and kingly name of the Imperial Crown of this Realm, in contempt of our said Lady the Queen and her laws, to the evil example of all others in the like case offending, contrary to the duty of the allegiance of him, the said Louis Riel, against the form of the statute in such case made and provided, and against the peace of our said Lady the Queen, her Crown and dignity.

"2. And the said Alexander David Stewart further saith: That the said Louis Riel, being a subject of our Lady the Queen, not regarding the duty of his allegiance, nor having the fear of God in his heart, but being moved and seduced by the instigation of the devil, as a false traitor against our Lady the Queen, and wholly withdrawing the allegiance, fidelity and obedience which every true and faithful subject of our said Lady the Queen should and of right ought to bear towards our said Lady the Queen, on the twenty-fourth day of April, in the year aforesaid, together with divers other false traitors, to the said Alexander David Stewart unknown, armed and arrayed in a warlike manner, that is to say, with guns, rifles, pistols, bayonets and other weapons, being then unlawfully, maliciously and traitorously assembled and gathered together against our said Lady the Queen, most wickedly, maliciously and traitorously did levy and make war against our said Lady the Queen, at the locality known as Fish Creek, in the said the North-West Territories of Canada, and within this Realm, and did then maliciously and traitorously attempt and endeavour by force and arms to subvert and destroy the constitution and government of this Realm, as by law established, and deprive and depose our said Lady the Queen of and from the style, honour and kingly name of the Imperial Crown of this Realm, in contempt of our said Lady the Queen and her laws, to the evil example of all others in the like case offending, contrary to the duty of the allegiance of him, the said Louis Riel, against the form of the statute in such case made and provided, and against the peace of our said Lady the Queen, her Crown and dignity.

" 3. And the said Alexander David Stewart further saith: That the said Louis Riel, being a subject of our Lady the Queen, not regarding the duty of his allegiance, nor having the fear of God in his heart, but being moved and seduced by the instigation of the devil, as a traitor against our said Lady the Queen, and wholly withdrawing the allegiance, fidelity and obedience which every true and faithful subject of our said Lady the Queen should and of right ought to bear towards our said Lady the Queen, on the ninth, tenth, eleventh and twelfth days of May, in the year aforesaid, together with divers other false traitors, to the said Alexander David Stewart unknown, armed and arrayed in a warlike manner, that is to say, with guns, rifles, pistols, bayonets and other weapons, being then unlawfully, maliciously and traitorously assembled and gathered together against our said Lady the Queen, most wickedly, maliciously and traitorously did levy and make war against our said Lady the Queen, at the locality known as Batoche, in the said the North-West Territories of Canada, within this Realm, and did then maliciously and traitorously attempt and endeavour, by force and arms, to subvert and destroy the constitution and government of this Realm, as by law established, and deprive and depose our said Lady the Queen of and from the style, honour and kingly name of the Imperial Crown of this Realm, in contempt of our said Lady the Queen and her laws, to the evil example of all others in like case offending,

contrary to the duty of the allegiance of him, the said Louis
Riel, against the form of the statute in such case made and
provided, and against the peace of our said Lady the Queen,
her Crown and dignity.

"4. And the said Alexander David Stewart further saith:
That the said Louis Riel, then *living within the Dominion of
Canada and under the protection of our Sovereign Lady the
Queen**, not regarding the duty of his allegiance, nor having
the fear of God in his heart, but being moved and seduced by the
instigation of the devil, as a false traitor against our said Lady
the Queen, and wholly withdrawing the allegiance, fidelity
and obedience which he should and of right ought to bear
towards our said Lady the Queen, on the twenty-sixth day of
March, in the year aforesaid, together with divers other false
traitors, to the said Alexander David Stewart unknown,
armed and arrayed in a warlike manner, that is to say, with
guns, rifles, pistols, bayonets and other weapons, being then
unlawfully, maliciously and traitorously assembled and gathered together against our said Lady the Queen, most wickedly, maliciously and traitorously did levy and make war
against our said Lady the Queen, at the locality known as
Duck Lake, in the said the North-West Territories of Canada,
and within this Realm, and did then maliciously and traitorously attempt and endeavour by force and arms to subvert and
destroy the constitution and government of this Realm, as
by law established, and deprive and depose our said Lady
the Queen of and from the style, honour and kingly name of
the Imperial Crown of this Realm, in contempt of our said
Lady the Queen and her laws, to the evil example of all others
in like case offending, contrary to the duty of the allegiance of
him, the said Louis Riel, against the form of the statute in
such case made and provided, and against the peace of our
said Lady the Queen, her Crown and dignity.

"5. And the said Alexander David Stewart further saith:

---

* The *Italics* are mine.

That the said Louis Riel, then living within the Dominion of Canada, and under the protection of our Sovereign Lady the Queen, not regarding the duty of his allegiance, nor having the fear of God in his heart, but being moved and seduced by the instigation of the devil, as a false traitor against our said Lady the Queen, and wholly withdrawing the allegiance, fidelity and obedience which he should and of right ought to bear towards our said Lady the Queen, on the twenty-fourth day of April, in the year aforesaid, together with divers other false traitors, to the said Alexander David Stewart unknown, armed and arrayed in a warlike manner, that is to say, with guns, rifles, pistols, bayonets and other weapons, being then unlawfully, maliciously and traitorously assembled and gathered together against our said Lady the Queen, most wickedly, maliciously and traitorously did levy and make war against our said Lady the Queen, at the locality known as Fish Creek, in the said the North-West Territories of Canada, and within this Realm, and did then maliciously and traitorously attempt and endeavour by force and arms to subvert and destroy the constitution and government of this Realm, as by law established, and deprive and depose our said Lady the Queen of and from the style, honour and kingly name of the Imperial Crown of this Realm, in contempt of our said Lady the Queen and her laws, to the evil example of all others in like case offending, contrary to the allegiance of him, the said Louis Riel, against the form of the statute in such case made and provided, and against the peace of our said Lady the Queen, her Crown and dignity.

" 6. And the said Alexander David Stewart further saith: That the said Louis Riel, then living within the Dominion of Canada, and under the protection of Our Sovereign Lady the Queen, not regarding the duty of his allegiance, nor having the fear of God in his heart, but being moved and seduced by the instigation of the devil, as a false traitor against our said Lady the Queen, and wholly withdrawing the allegiance, fidelity and obedience which he should and of right ought to bear towards our said Lady the Queen, on the ninth, tenth, eleventh and twelfth days of May, in the year aforesaid, together with divers other false traitors, to the said Alexander David Stewart unknown, armed and arrayed in a warlike manner, that is to say, with guns, rifles, pistols, bayonets and other weapons, being then unlawfully, maliciously and traitorously assembled and gathered together against our said Lady the Queen, most wickedly and maliciously and traitorously did levy and make war against our said Lady the Queen, at the locality known as Batoche, in the said the North-West Territories of Canada and within this Realm, and did then maliciously and traitorously attempt and endeavour by force and arms to subvert and destroy the constitution and government of this Realm, as by law established, and deprive and depose our said Lady the Queen of and from the style, honour and kingly name of the Imperial Crown of this Realm, in contempt of our said Lady the Queen and her laws, to the evil example of others in like case offending, contrary to the duty of allegiance of him, the said Louis Riel, against the form of the statute in such case made and provided, and against the peace of our said Lady the Queen, her crown and dignity."

[Signed]   " A. D. STEWART."

Sworn before me, the day and year first above mentioned, at the town of Regina, in the North-West Territories of Canada.

[Signed]   HUGH RICHARDSON,
A Stipendiary Magistrate
In and for the North-West Territories of Canada.

APPENDIX E.

[*Open Letter of Louis Riel, Published in the Irish World of November 21, 1885.*]

[The following is one of the most scathing arraignments of British tyranny ever published, since the day Junius indicted his celebrated letter to the king.]

To the Citizens of the United States of America.

FELLOW-MEN:—The outside world has heard but little of my people since the beginning of this war in the North-West Territory, and that little has been related by agents and apologists of the bloodthirsty British Empire. As of old, England's infernal machination of *Falsehood* has been employed to defame our character, to misrepresent our motives, and to brand our soldiers and allies as cruel savages. These things I learn from American papers, which come to me through the same channel that I send this to you. The end which our enemies have in view is plain. Their object is to prevent good people from extending to us their sympathy while they themselves may rob us in the dark and murder us without pity.

Of one hundred or more papers that now lie in my tent, *The Irish World,* I find, is the only true friend we have. In the columns of this far-famed journal, the truth is fully told. England's organs in the United States and Canada falsely aver that my people have no grievances. To contradict their false statements, I now write to the defender of the oppressed,

Mr. Patrick Ford, whose *Irish World* will publish a true statement of the facts in all corners of the globe.

Our lands in the North-West Territory, the possession of which was solemnly confirmed by government fifteen years ago, have since been torn from us, and given to land-grabbers who never saw the country—and this after we had cut down forests, plucked up stumps, removed rocks, ploughed and seeded the soil, and built substantial homes for ourselves and our children.

Nearly all the good, available lands in this territory (as is the case with the lands East of the Rocky Mountains) are already in the clutches of English lords, who have large herds of cattle grazing thereon; and the riches which these lands produce are drained out of the country and sent over to England to be consumed by a people that fatten on a system that pauperizes us.

This wholesale robbery and burglary has been carried on, and is still carried on, with the connivance of accursed England. The result is extermination or slavery. Against this monstrous tyranny we have been forced to rebel. It is not in human nature to quietly acquiesce in it.

In their treatment of us, however, the behaviour of the English is not singular. Follow those pirates the world over, and you will find that everywhere, and at all times, they adopt the same tactics, and operate on the same thievish lines.

Ireland, India, the Highlands of Scotland, Australia, and the isles of the Indian Ocean—all these countries are the sad evidences, and their native populations are the witnesses of England's land-robberies.

Even in the United States—and it is a burning shame for the government and the people of that great and free nation to have it to be said—English lords have, within a few short years, grabbed territory enough to form several large states. Alas! for the people of your country! Alas! for the government for whose independence and glory the soldiers of George

Washington fought bare-foot against the cut-throats and hell-hounds of England! Alas! that this same evil power should be allowed to return and reconquer so much of your nation without a shot being fired or even a word of protest being uttered in the name of the American people!

Your government, which has allowed her citizens to be robbed of their heritage by English lords and English capitalists, has also given aid and comfort to the English in permitting her General* Howard to come to Manitoba and the North-West Territory to school the assassins that were sent from Toronto to murder me and my people, and to give the Queen's Own lessons in handling the American Gatling gun, as well as in granting license to British soldiers and British ammunition intended for our destruction to pass over American soil. By its conduct in this entire business the administration at Washington has made the United States the ally of England in fighting a people who are fighting only for homes and firesides. Does it require two powerful nations, such as the United States and England, to put down the Saskatchewan rebellion? Grover Cleveland and Secretary Bayard have much to answer for.

It is now evident, as *The Irish World* has charged, that these two high officials of the United States are more English than American. The animus they have shown towards my people and me for the past two months, as well as the friendship and aid they have extended to our enemies, is but an additional confirmation of what has been charged against them.

Can it be possible that the American people, or any considerable portion of them, have any real sympathy with England? Have they not read, has it not come down to them from bleeding sire to son, of the crimes and the atrocities and fiendish cruelties which that wicked power inflicted upon

---

* Riel was mistaken. This creature was not a general; neither was he a soldier of our government.

their patriotic fathers during the Revolution? Of the American towns wantonly given to the flames by order of English commanders; of the horrors of the English prison ships, and the barbarities imposed by the English upon American prisoners of war? Does not American history record the outrages perpetrated by England upon American commerce and American citizenship which led to the war of 1812? And is it not still fresh in the memory of men of middle age how, when the republic was engaged in a life-and-death struggle with the slave-holders' rebellion, England gloated over your troubles and sent her sympathy and her money and her armed ships to your enemies to destroy your Union and to bring the American name in disgrace before the world? Generous minds forgive injuries, but spaniels lick the hand that smites them. The Americans are not spaniels; but there are sycophants and lickspittles in America, nevertheless, and those base natures are but to the honest people of to-day what the Tories were to the honest and patriotic people a century ago. They are not Americans.

A word here to the French and Irish of Canada, and I am done: I beg and pray, that they will not allow themselves to be induced by any threats or by any blandishments to come out against us. Our cause is just, and therefore no just man of any race or nationality ought to stand opposed to us. The enemies who seek our destruction are strangers to justice. They are cruel, treacherous and bloody. And yet, like the tiger, they are only obeying the instincts of their nature. But for the Irish people, who for centuries have been robbed and massacred and hunted from their island home by the English, and whose good name is reviled by the English in all lands, or for the Canadian French, who are subjected to the grossest and most ruffianly abuse from the same, to aid in any way these enemies would be not only wrong but stupid and unnatural.

In a little while it will be all over. We may fail. But the

rights for which we contend will not die. A day of reckoning will come to our enemies and of jubilee to my people. The hated yoke of English domination and arrogance will be broken in this land, and the long-suffering victims of their injustice will, with God's blessing, re-enter into the peaceful enjoyments of their possessions.

LOUIS RIEL.

BATOCHE, N. W. T., *May 6, 1885.*

11

APPENDIX F.

———

———

[TRANSLATION.]

WASHINGTON, D. C., *August 24, 1885.*

DEAR FRIEND GAGNON—The journals which I have received during the past two days, indicate that there is great diversity of views among our Canadian journalists in the United States in regard to the rights which American citizenship confers upon Louis Riel, in his present unfortunate situation. I notice, too, that public meetings are being held, and petitions signed, and that these meetings and petitions are not agreed upon the best method to proceed to arrest the execution. Evidently there is danger that the generous, humane action of our people may be devoid of influence, by reason of the diversity of views expressed or the poverty of the arguments advanced in the memorials addressed to our government, asking its interference in Riel's case.

Being desirous to ascertain the views of the Department of State in regard to this matter, so as to satisfy myself, and, if opportunity afforded, be of service to my compatriots, I called on Secretary Bayard this afternoon to talk over the matter with him. We discussed the subject together at considerable length. From our interview I can say that the following is substantially the views of the department of state; of course the form in which it is expressed is my own:

First. The American government will not take the initiative in examining into Riel's citizenship or the rights thereunder.*

———

* This absurdity is without precedent, and devoid of common sense.

Second. The government has so far done nothing in the matter, except to inquire of the War Department as to the truth or falsity of a statement to the effect that Riel was captured on American soil. This information was asked for to reply to a New York correspondent who inquired concerning the matter. The secretary read me his reply, which is unimportant.

Third. The government will take no action in the case, unless the matter is presented to its attention in a formal manner, the facts and arguments upon which the interference of the government is invoked to be properly stated in writing.

Fourth. The government would not be disposed to inquire into or review the proceedings of the court which tried Riel, unless it was shown that he was discriminated against, *i. e.*, that he was tried by harsher methods than a Canadian citizen would have been tried by.*

Fifth. The government recognizes the principle that every country has a right to determine for itself what constitutes treason, and it would not be disposed to question Canada's right to try Riel for treason even though he be a native or naturalized citizen of the United States. I understand the secretary to say that Riel's case was like some of the Irish so-called revolutionists, so far as it regards this government, and that the American government would do all that was proper for Riel as it had done for the others.

With these views of the department of state before us it seems to me that our duty is traced more clearly.

You are aware that I knew Riel intimately both before and after his becoming insane. Knowing the material he is made of, as well as his intimate views and aspirations, I believe that *when he gave himself up* (when he could have escaped with Dumont) *he did so with the determined pur-*

---

* It is presumed, that if Canadian courts were in the habit of using torture in the trial of Canucks, Secretary Bayard would not object to their using it upon American citizens resident in Canada.

pose of having himself put to death as the best means of serving his people and country. I am of the opinion that in madness he acted with an extreme sagacity which he might have been devoid of with his wits. If Riel is executed, mark me! the children of his executors, in the not-distant future, will erect monuments to his memory. You know the history of Pontiac! Riel is the Pontiac of the XIX. century.

Yours Truly,

EDMOND MALLET.

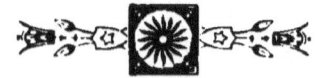

APPENDIX G.

———

[*Copy of Letter from Major Edmond Mallet to Mr. Thomas D. Rambaut.*]

———

February 9, 1886.

Thomas D. Rambaut, Esq., New York, N. Y.

DEAR SIR:—Your note finds me on the eve of my departure from the city for a few days, and in the midst of such occupations that is really impossible for me to find the newspaper articles which appeared relative to my efforts to have the U. S. Government interfere in the Riel case. I will now give you the substance of what was done, and if that does not quite answer your purpose, let me know, and I will give you fuller indications next week.

I first consulted Mr. Bayard, and he took this position, substantially:

(1) That it was not the duty of the government to inquire into the fact of Riel's American citizenship, and (2) that the government could not interfere even if he was an American citizen, either natural or adopted. If a *case* was brought to the attention of his department it would be examined into, but under no circumstances could the government, he thought, interfere, unless it was shown conclusively that he had been discriminated against during his trial by reason of his American citizenship.

When it became apparent to me that the Canadian Government had committed itself to the execution of Riel, under the pressure brought to bear upon it by the Orange lodges of Ontario, I went to the president and appealed to him to prevent this judicial murder. I based my appeal on the following: (1) That Riel was an *American* citizen, that he had been indicted as a *British* citizen, his American citizenship having been entirely ignored, although offer had been made to prove the fact by documents captured at the battle of Batoche, and then in the Canadian Government's hands, and that he had been tried by a half jury of six men, selected by the judge, and that judge was a mere justice of the peace; (2) that Riel was insane; and I offered testimony to that effect; and (3) that the authority to put a human being to death for any cause whatsoever is not inherited in government, but is delegated from God, and that such delegated power can be exercised only in certain conditions, such as sound mind, etc. The president seemed much interested in the case, expressed himself in sympathy with what I told him; but he considered it a very grave matter to interfere. At last I asked that he send for Mr. Bayard and the British minister, and see if an amicable understanding could be made to save Riel. The president then said he would consult with the secretary of state and see what could be done. During the night of the same day the Associated Press announced that, to my appeal, the president had been constrained to decline interfering in the matter.

Respectfully Yours,
EDMOND MALLET.

APPENDIX H.

ST. PETER'S MISSION, ST. PETER P. O., MONTANA, *Jan. 14, 1887.*
Mr. Wilbur F. Bryant, Judge, West Point, Nebr.

DEAR SIR:—Your favor at hand and in reply I would say that Louis Riel was here just prior to the North-West Rebellion and he left this place at the request of a delegation composed of three half-breed men, who came after him from their northern country. He lived here about six months. He was married to a half-breed girl called Marguerite Monete from whom he had two children: John, born 9th May, 1882, and Mary Angelica, born 11th Sept., 1883. The girl was born here, and the boy somewhere down the Missouri or Musselshell while Riel was living on the prairie among the half-breeds. Politics was his principal thought, [you] might say, and in the last years from the democrat [he] passed to the republican party. Sun River is a small place and he lived not in town, but here around the Mission, which is about 20 miles distant from Sun River. He was making his living teaching school and [it] would have been better for him, as he was told, to stick at it and retire entirely from all politics; but his mind was changed there, and this brought the unfortunate man to such a frightful end. With kindest regards, I remain

Yours Respectfully,
J. DAMIENS, *S. J.*

APPENDIX I.

[*Letter from Colonel Hugh Richardson, the Stipendiary Magistrate Who Tried Riel.*]

REGINA, *26th April, 1887.*

MY DEAR SIR:—I reply to the queries contained in your letter of 21st inst., received here to-day.

The officer charged with the execution of "Riel" was the sheriff of the N. W. T., the actual duty, as I have understood, being performed by his deputy, under the sheriff's supervision. Who the hangman was I know not, nor is it known beyond a sort of rumour that one Henderson so acted, and [as to] whether or not this man had been a prisoner of Riel's in the earlier rebellion, I am ignorant. I was not in the country until 1876, and except traveling through the Red River country on my way West, and an occasional visit to Winnipeg since '76, I know but little of the people.

There is, or was not long since, a man John Henderson here, who is a half-breed hailing from Red River, a freighter by occupation, and also a guide, having formerly, it is said, been a plain hunter. The duty of "executing the law," however, devolves by express statute upon the sheriff.

In the winter of 1884 a gallows was erected for the execution of two men: Stevenson, who suffered the penalty for the murder of a settler. This, as I have been told, was used again in '85, when Connor was hanged, and later in the execution of Riel, and still subsists as part of the "public gaol paraphernalia."   Yours, Very Truly,

HUGH RICHARDSON.

APPENDIX J.

ERRATA ET CÆTERA.

---

1. At page 12, supply "the" before the proper name "Belly."

2. At page 38, for "Cotta" read "Cottu."

3. At page 65, for "Bellimense" read "Bellimeure."

4. At page 79, for "uptopian" read "utopian."

5. At page 81, for "isoseles" read "isosceles."

6. At page 84, for "coulee-ravine" (as a compound word) read "coulee—ravine," (separated with dash), the entire expression: "Ravine, with stream running through it," being the appositive of "coulee."

7. At page 85, for "Marchard" read "Marchand."

8. At page 94, for "four hundred and seven" read "five hundred and eighty-four, inclusive of non-combatants."

9. The great bay in the north-eastern part of our continent is commonly called Hudson's Bay, and its outlet Hudson's Strait. I have adopted the names "Hudson Bay" and "Hudson Strait," sanctioned, as I believe, by good usage.

12

www.ingramcontent.com/pod-product-compliance
Lightning Source LLC
Chambersburg PA
CBHW031117020726
47495CB00007B/2240